# BLAMELESS

# BLAMELESS

*a novel*

## THOM LEMMONS

WATERBROOK
PRESS

BLAMELESS
PUBLISHED BY WATERBROOK PRESS
12265 Oracle Boulevard, Suite 200
Colorado Springs, Colorado 80921
*A division of Random House Inc.*

Scripture quotations are taken from the Holy Bible, New International Version®.
NIV®. Copyright © 1973, 1978, 1984 by International Bible Society. Used by
permission of Zondervan Publishing House. All rights reserved.

All quotations from Nathaniel Hawthorne's *The Scarlet Letter* are from the online text
facsimile of the original Ticknor and Fields edition of 1850, found at www.eldritch
press.org/nh/sl.html. This edition is in the public domain. Note the following state-
ment from the Web master of the above site: "In order to allow the fullest possible
reuse of these works we have dedicated them to the public domain under a Creative
Commons deed." See http://new.creativecommons.org:9000/licenses/eldred-pd.

ISBN 978-1-4000-7174-6

Library of Congress Cataloging-in-Publication Data
Lemmons, Thom.
    Blameless : a novel / Thom Lemmons. — 1st ed.
        p. cm.
    ISBN-13: 978-1-4000-7174-6
    1. College teachers—Fiction. 2. Literature teachers—Fiction. I. Title.
    PS3562.E474B55 2007
    813'.54—dc22
                                    2006031248

Printed in the United States of America
2007—First Edition

10 9 8 7 6 5 4 3 2 1

*To Karla, la más bonita*

The metaphor is probably the most fertile power possessed by man.

—JOSÉ ORTEGA Y GASSET, philosopher

The folly of mistaking a paradox for a discovery,
a metaphor for a proof, a torrent of verbiage for a spring
of capital truths, and oneself for an oracle, is inborn in us.

—PAUL VALÉRY, poet

I had a strong sense that God doesn't care so much
about being analyzed. Mainly, he wants to be loved.

—PHILIP YANCEY

Later I passed by, and when I looked at you
and saw that you were old enough for love, I spread the corner
of my garment over you and covered your nakedness.
I gave you my solemn oath and entered into a covenant with you,
declares the Sovereign LORD, and you became mine.

—EZEKIEL 16:8

I'm just saying he's not everything you think he is, that's all."

Alexis sighed and closed her eyes. Why did she allow Lucy to pull her into these conversations? "And how would you know what I think he is?"

Lucy sat at her desk, primly tapping at her keyboard, her lips compressed into the tight, holier-than-thou stamp of disapproval that inevitably made Alexis want to throw something. She stared at Lucy for a long time, long enough that she finally decided the conversation was over.

She should have known better. As she turned toward her office door, Lucy said, "I'm only thinking of you, Dr. Hartnett."

Alexis turned slowly to face Lucy. "What's that supposed to mean?"

*Tap, tap, tap.* "Oh, just…you know. This campus is like a small town. People talk."

"And what do they say?"

"Now, don't get all upset—"

"I asked you a question."

"I'm just the messenger, Dr. Hartnett."

"Fine. What's the message?"

In the silence that followed, Alexis could hear the ticking of the second hand on the wall clock behind Lucy's desk. Despite herself, she began to count the ticks. She was up to twelve when Lucy gave her a guilty look and cleared her throat with a noise that sounded to Alexis like an actual "ahem."

"It's just…some people in the departments… That is, I've heard…"

"Lucy, why don't you just tell me what you've got against Dr. Barnes?"

Lucy looked at her, and for an instant, Alexis could have sworn she saw something like anger in her administrative assistant's eyes. "Dr. Hartnett, everybody knows the university is in a budget crunch. And you've missed the last two deadlines from the provost for your final allocation requests. You have a lot to think about these days, and I think you ought to ask yourself if you're really focused on the College of Arts and Humanities, or…or something else."

So. There it was, out in the open. Or as close to the open as Lucy was likely to venture.

Lucy was efficient, reliable, punctual, responsible…and, at times, thoroughly irritating. For some reason, Alexis habitually thought of her as older—from a previous generation, even—though Alexis knew Lucy was probably about her age. She had been the dean's administrative assistant before Alexis had occupied this position. As far as she could see, Lucy appeared from nowhere each morning and disappeared the same way each evening after work. Alexis had never heard her mention friends, family, co-workers—none of the normal small talk that usually oiled the wheels of days and weeks spent in the same working space.

Lucy was the master of the emotional Trojan horse. You got mad at yourself because you didn't know how to get mad at her; she gave you no fingerholds. Alexis now asked herself, *was* she thinking about something else? Did Lucy, in fact, have a point? Did Lucy suspect that in Alexis's more self-aware moments, she had noticed she was thinking of Joe Barnes in those little, out-of-the-way instants scattered randomly in her life, like the corners in her house that accumulated dust, unnoticed until a mother-in-law's visit?

Drinking her juice in the morning, Alexis would catch herself wondering what he was having for breakfast. Or in the middle of a committee meeting, she would think of him in his classroom, trying, in that kind, nonblaming way he had, to inch his students toward knowledge. And anytime she ran across a passage from Hawthorne…

Alexis dug in her heels. She was going to give Lucy an answer, so she grabbed the first one that seemed handy.

"Lucy, I hardly know the man. I don't see what all the fuss is about."

Lucy shrugged but kept her eyes on Alexis's face. "Well, then. Fine."

"Fine."

Lucy nodded and shrugged again—probably for emphasis, Alexis guessed.

Alexis went into her office. Maybe the door shut behind her a trifle harder than she had intended. She sat down at her desk and sifted through the stack of papers on her blotter: a memo from the VP of finance, reminding all deans that budgets for the next year were due in a week and a half; a printout of the registration numbers for the semester—slightly below budget, as usual; an abstract of the latest departmental self-studies, which she was supposed to sell to the accreditation team coming in next month; and yet another copy of the proofs for the college's new brochure, with a plea attached—slightly more urgent than the one paper-clipped to the proofs she'd received three days ago—for her final comments and approval. Then there were the manila file folders stacked on the front edge of her desk. Alexis looked at them for a few seconds and shuffled the papers again. She spread them across her blotter with the idea of putting the most urgent one on the left and working her way to the right.

It was no use; Lucy had successfully planted the burr under her saddle. Or, more accurately, she had reminded Alexis of the persistent, low-grade irritation of a burr that had been there for longer than she was willing to admit.

Alexis swiveled her chair to stare out across the quadrangle. She watched the students ambling to and from class. A couple passed just below her window, draped around each other. For an instant she wished the dean of students would make good on his threats to put some teeth in the dress codes. At least the slouchy jeans and haphazard hair might actually stand for something. But then guilt hushed her inner neoconservative. Though her undergrad days at Berkeley ended in 1971, she had never quite managed the reverse pilgrimage to the right made by many of her peers. A part of her still believed in "power to the people," even though the last couple of decades had demonstrated to her that most people were more interested in comfort than empowerment. Especially the couple walking past her window.

Alexis looked at the pair in their loose T-shirts, flip-flops peeking with each shuffling step from beneath the ragged, trailing edges of their denim pants. Maybe what she was feeling was a sort of wistful longing. She could understand the wish for comfort. A little soothing company once in a while, an occasional oasis of congenial companionship could go a long way. She guessed that was close to the center of what lodged Joe so firmly in her mind: he seemed to offer comfort—at least when she watched him interact with his students, he did. Each time she heard him speak, the sound of his voice evidenced engagement and interest: in his students, history, politics, literary conversation, and—she sometimes dared to think—in her. It had been a long time since she'd seen anything like a spark in a man's eye, but with Joe... Well, she thought it was possible at least.

*Probably the imaginings of a spring chicken who's staring down the muzzle of late October.*

*Oh, Dr. B.,* she thought, *why did you wander across the stage of my life right when I was almost comfortable with the idea of a gradual slide into retirement, Tuesday-afternoon bridge, and no surprises?*

# ONE

Tielman fumed, standing outside Joe's door. What a lousy night to be out doing a favor for a guy whose music was so loud he couldn't hear the doorbell!

"Come on, Joe! Turn it down already!"

Again Tielman slammed his fist against the door, staring uselessly through the pane at the back of Joe's head. Tielman could hear the brassy roaring of an orchestra and chorus coming through the locked door. He might as well be sending smoke signals. He slapped his palm against the door.

"Joe, open up for Pete's sake."

With his luck, Tielman figured the neighbors would call in a complaint about the guy making all the noise in the stairwell outside 777.

Miraculously, Joe's head swiveled toward the front door. He squinted, smiled, gave Tielman a little wave, and aimed a remote at his CD player. The tidal wave of sound vanished.

The deadbolt snicked back, the door swung open, and Joe reached for Tielman's hand, pulling him into the apartment.

"Hey, Al! Man, it's cold out there. What are you doing standing outside? Come on in."

"I'd have come in about five minutes earlier if you hadn't cranked your stereo up to the pain threshold."

Joe gave a sheepish grin. "Sorry, Al. But you can't listen to the Verdi *Requiem* at low volume."

Tielman slid off his gloves and stuffed them into his coat pockets. "How about something from the Windham Hill catalog—George Winston maybe? Especially on an evening when it's freaking cold and you're expecting a guest." He shrugged out of the coat and handed it to Joe.

"How about some coffee?" Joe said, tossing the coat through a bedroom doorway.

"Yeah, great."

Tielman sat on the couch. Joe had his place set up pretty well, especially for a guy who wasn't married. Lots of solid-color fabric upholstery and pillows decorated with subtle patterns. Framed art prints on the walls. Blond wood bookshelves that looked like something from one of those online decorating stores. Canned uplighting in the corners. A tasteful blend of Pier 1 and Crate & Barrel.

"You sure you're not gay?" he said as Joe handed him a steaming mug.

"We're college teachers, Al. Stereotypes are off-limits, remember?"

"This place is so organized, though. How do you ever get anything done?"

"Concentration, my friend. Pure concentration."

"This what you were talking about?" Tielman picked up the sheaf of papers lying on the cushion between them.

"Yeah, I was just looking it over."

The double-spaced text was hash-marked with editing notations; both margins bore scribbled notes.

"I'd like to get your impressions before I redraft it for submission," Joe said. "I'm the new guy around here; I figure you can help me avoid the shoals."

"Wouldn't guarantee it, but…"

Tielman scanned the cover page. *Between Heaven and Earth: Shame, Grace, and Redemption in the Writing of Nathaniel Hawthorne. A proposal submitted by Dr. Joseph Barnes…*

He looked up at Joe. "Your dissertation was on Hawthorne, right?"

"Yeah."

"I thought I remembered that from your CV. So why do you need me? You're the department expert."

Joe laughed and ran a hand through his hair, shoving a thick, graying lock out of his face. "Well, it was a long time ago, Al, and I haven't done much on him since. You know how it is with faculty committees: you can gore somebody's ox without even knowing it. I don't need to get off to that kind of start."

*True enough,* Al thought. There were still some sore feelings among the deconstructionist cadre at the end of the hall over the approval of a summer stipend for one of the assistant professors to go to England to research a new biography on C. S. Lewis. Tielman thought he was never going to be able to enter the faculty commons again without having to listen to five or six nasal choruses about the department's regrettable lack of commitment to the postmodern ethic. Bunch of misplaced philosophy hacks.

"Why'd you let Hawthorne drop, then?"

Joe stared into an empty place just over Tielman's head. He wore a funny little half smile. He opened his mouth, then closed it again, finally shaking his head. "I can't really go into that with you now, Al. There isn't time."

Tielman gave him a sideways look. "Whatever, man. It's just words on a page."

Joe wouldn't look at him. "Yeah, Al. That's all it ever is."

Tielman shrugged and flipped through the pages of the abstract for a couple of minutes. He felt the vague beginnings of discomfort that usually came when thoughtful silence descended. Long gaps had never been his preferred conversational moments. He had the sense such wasn't the case with Joe. When Tielman couldn't stand it any longer, he cleared his throat and gestured at the page he was reading.

"You might tighten the language here a little bit. And this stuff about constructive remorse as a declining fashion is probably a little heavy handed too. Or could seem that way to certain people."

"Too preachy?"

"Yeah."

Joe nodded. "I can see that. Some years ago one of my students compared me to Harold Bloom."

"No kidding? What I wouldn't give for a student who'd even heard of Harold Bloom."

Joe grinned. "On the course-end evaluation, he said I was 'too sure of the correctness of my conclusions to permit honest, intellectual inquiry.'"

"You aesthetic Nazi, you."

"Probably overstated his case. But you have to admit, Jonathan Edwards isn't getting many party invitations these days."

"Which brings us back to Hawthorne."

"Yeah."

"I don't see anything here that's too far out of whack. Your edits and notations are on, for the most part. I'd say just redraft it, get a couple of readers to look it over, and you're ready to present."

"Okay, great. Need more coffee?"

Tielman stared into his cup for a few seconds. "Decaf?"

"You kidding? This late? Of course."

"Are we really turning into our fathers?"

"That or our mothers," Joe said. He took Tielman's mug and walked toward the kitchenette.

"Just a half," Tielman said as Joe reached for the coffeepot. "I told Barbara I'd be home in time for dinner."

"Hey, take off if you need to. You've already been tons of help."

"Nah, I can stay a couple more minutes."

"Okay. Say, you think you could recommend a couple of readers for this once I'm ready?"

Tielman reached for the mug. "Bill Schuman has a good sense of what the committee's looking for, and he did some work in nineteenth-century American lit before he specialized in medieval. And, um… Sophie Namath maybe. Wouldn't be bad to have a woman look this over. Sophie's got inclusive-language radar."

"Sounds great. I'll talk to them."

Tielman slurped some coffee. His eyes roved Joe's bookshelves. "Ayn Rand, Eudora Welty, Kate Chopin, Joyce Carol Oates… Why didn't they get you to teach the women's lit section?"

Joe gave a little smile and wagged his finger. "Stereotypes, Al."

"Regular Alan Alda. How'd a sensitive, straight guy like you stay single all these years?"

Joe stood up and walked toward the kitchenette. "Sure I can't get you some more coffee?"

Tielman raised his eyebrows and watched Joe's retreating back. "Hey, Joe, I didn't mean—"

Joe gave a tight little shake of the head. "Forget it." He lifted the coffeepot toward Tielman with a questioning look.

"No, really. I've gotta go." Tielman set his mug on the kitchenette counter. He crossed to the bedroom and retrieved his overcoat. He slid his arms into the sleeves and fastened the buttons, then dug in the pockets for his gloves. Joe was still standing by the coffeepot, staring at the countertop.

"Say, Joe, Barbara and I keep meaning to have you over. She can't cook anything to speak of, but she loves Hawthorne—no kidding. And I can toss on some steaks or something."

Joe tugged his eyes away from the countertop. He was a little slow on the draw with the smile he showed. "Yeah, sure, Al. That'd be great."

"Okay, well… Guess I'd better get going."

Bracing himself for the blast, Tielman tugged on the door. *Poor guy. Wonder what her name was.*

He clutched his collar, ducked his head, and jogged toward the parking lot. As he navigated against the biting wind, he had a vague sense that he ought to warn Joe about something…but he didn't know what.

Maybe it had something to do with that open, vulnerable moment following Al's chance remark about Joe's being single. Clearly, there was a wound that hadn't healed. It was none of Al's business, of course. But he couldn't help wondering…

Joe was fabulous in the classroom, no doubt about that. On the few occasions Al had passed his doorway, the kids seemed focused, involved—as much as kids did these days. Joe Barnes was clearly an asset to the department. And there was no reason a guy like him shouldn't be on the tenure track; a Thomson fellowship would be just the thing to get him moving along.

But something was nagging at Al. A guy like Joe who looked so good, both on paper and in person... Maybe it was just superstition, but Al had a feeling something was bound to go wrong. It made no sense, and he promised himself that as soon as he got home, he'd rinse the notion out of his mind with a glass of something or other.

He got in his car and slammed the door, cursing the cold under his breath. He backed out of the parking space, then gave a final glance at the brightly lit windows of Joe's apartment. He shook his head and drove off into the night.

⁂

"So, what are the connections between the Twain of, say, *Huckleberry Finn* and the Twain of *Letters from the Earth*?"

Joe waited. Eventually the silence would flush somebody out. Yes, there: front row, left side. The serious girl who always wore socks with her sandals.

"Yes, Portia?"

"Well, Dr. Barnes, it seems to me that *Letters from the Earth* is more about Twain's cynicism toward religion than anything else. I mean, there's a little of it in *Huckleberry Finn,* but, like, um..."

*Such a promising start, Portia. An A for effort...*

"Okay, the cynicism, sure. We see hints of it in the earlier work, don't we? Anybody think of an example?"

*Oh, come on, kids. Even if all you did was see that dreadful movie with Jonathan Taylor Thomas, you ought to be able to dredge up something.*

The jock in the back of the room. *Mirabile dictu!* "Yes, Jamal?"

"Well, uh, like…the king dude, he scams the people with religion."

"Good! Not just in *Huckleberry Finn* but in many of his short stories, Twain ridicules both religious shysters and the gullible people taken in by them. Great! What else?"

Joe kept poking and prodding, by turns cajoling and cheering them on, until the class's collective consciousness, moving with ameba-like grace and speed, subsumed the few concepts he had determined to introduce during today's session. He glanced at his watch.

"Okay, that's all the time we have today. Remember, your essays are due by the end of class Thursday," he said, raising his voice to ride above the sound of books slamming and backpacks being unzipped. "Oh, and if you haven't decided on an author for your midterm profile, be sure to see me by the end of the week. The list is in your syllabus."

Joe tucked his notes into his valise. He sucked in a deep breath and let it puff out his cheeks.

"Good day, huh?"

She was standing in the doorway, smiling at him in that offhanded way that he found so unaccountably affecting.

"Oh, hi. Well, I think we struck a few blows in defense of Brother Clemens's literary heritage."

"Well done. Freshman lit and comp isn't the terrain most favorable for such a battle."

He smiled at her and shrugged. "Ours is not to question why."

"Where are you headed?"

"Office hours, then lunch, I guess." He paused, then buried his eyes in his valise.

*Why don't you say it?*

"Well, I'll leave you to it," she said, starting to turn away.

*No. Don't let her get away—not yet.*

"What brings you around this way?" Joe picked up his valise and walked toward her, then flicked the light switch and closed the classroom door behind him.

"Oh, the newest mandate from the provost. We're supposed to be implementing the Sam Walton school of organizational supervision."

"Management by walking around?"

She shrugged and nodded.

"Any pointers?"

She shook her head and smiled at him, thrusting her hands into the side pockets of her blazer, and for an instant Joe saw with heartwarming clarity the young girl she had once been.

"No, I think you did an admirable job of tugging it out of them in there."

"Well, thank you. I consider that worthy praise, coming from my dean."

"Oh…why not think of it as coming from a friend?"

He looked at her, and her eyes didn't shy away. "All right. I think I like that even better."

She gave him a little wave. "Office hours, then."

"Yes."

He walked away, down the hall.

And then lunch—alone. *You despicable coward!*

⁂

She strolled back toward the administrative wing, trying to ignore the flush creeping up the back of her neck like steam crawling up a cold mirror. She felt brazen and foolish and young. What did she imagine she was doing, trolling his hallway just before the class break?

Something shoved against her shoulder, spinning her halfway around.

"Oh, my gosh! I'm sorry, Dr. Hartnett, I...I guess I wasn't paying attention..."

She collected herself and gave the shaggy-haired, stocking-capped boy what she hoped was a placid, guilt-free smile. "It's all right. Don't be late to class."

He gave her a quick nod, spun, and hurried off.

*Watch where you're going, old girl. Your bones aren't young enough to be mooning about in a busy hallway.*

## TWO

L ucy watched as Alexis came into the office. Lucy could tell she'd seen him or been with him or something. Lucy could always tell.

Alexis Hartnett was complicated. Competent, fair, tough, organized, sometimes generous to a fault...and complicated. And the one thing Lucy knew best about her, though it had always remained unspoken between them, was that Dr. Hartnett carried within her a deep openness to harm that made her one of the most careful people Lucy knew.

Lucy didn't know the reasons for the protections Alexis had erected around herself; she had never heard the story of their beginnings, nor was their relationship such that she would ever presume to ask. Even to acknowledge that she suspected the existence of some past circumstance that cast a shadow on Alexis's heart would be a violation of the tacit covenant between them. She was the dean's administrative assistant, not her counselor. Not even her friend, to be truthful.

But wasn't it part of her job to look out for her boss? Even if she left aside everything except her concern for the continued smooth functioning of the college, this budding obsession with Joe Barnes would spell trouble. Lucy had seen the memos from the provost and the president. She'd sent Alexis's responses and rebuttals, for crying out loud. The university wasn't exactly rolling in easy times. Anything that made Alexis less vigilant and efficient was bound to have some effect on Lucy too. Right?

Lucy thought about what she knew of Alexis. As a dean, she was tough, capable, and determined. She reminded Lucy of one of those female marathoners, getting on up in years but still lacing her shoes every day for the run. She was thin—but not desiccated, as so many middle-aged women became in the name of watching their weight— and her shoulders were square and carried always directly beneath her ears, as if she'd read one of those old handbooks of deportment for young women.

Lucy opened the top right drawer of her desk and reached for the small, square, resealable plastic container that she used to store her snacks. She peeled back the lid and withdrew a single toothpick-sized pretzel stick. She placed it on her tongue and began chewing, staring at the tiny digital clock in the bottom right corner of her computer screen. As she watched, it clicked over from 11:37 a.m. to 11:38. Another minute gone forever.

Alexis was divorced, and Lucy guessed she carried some scars from that. But didn't everyone carry scars from something or other?

Lucy was sure she did herself, though unlike many she could name, she never felt that gave her license to shirk her load.

Lucy could never decide whether she admired Alexis or was jealous of her. On one hand, she was an efficient administrator who enjoyed the loyalty of her subordinates and the respect of her superiors. On the other hand, there were those disturbing little chinks of vulnerability in the way her boss looked at someone or the tone of voice she used when speaking to a friend. Lucy wondered whether Alexis's vulnerability also conferred on her some sort of enhanced ability with people. That was what made Lucy jealous. Other people were certainly not Lucy's specialty.

Lucy reached for another pretzel stick and bit off one end with a small, precise snip. With her tongue, she felt the enamel-smooth baked shell in between the salt crystals stuck up and down the length of the pretzel.

People like Alexis needed to be protected from themselves, Lucy suspected. They needed shelter from the debris blown about on the wind of their own comings and goings.

"Lucy, where's the faculty renewal notebook? I thought you always kept it right here."

*How long has she been standing behind me? Note to self: no wool-gathering when the dean is in the office.* "Sorry, I didn't realize that's what you were looking for." Lucy closed the notebook that was lying open beside her computer screen, swiveled around in her chair, and held it out toward Alexis.

"What were you doing with it?"

"I'm making a spreadsheet of all the applications we've received so far. There's quite a bit of interest this time."

"Really? Well, I can wait until you're finished to—"

"No, that's fine. I have other projects to work on. Just put it back when you're through with it."

Alexis took the notebook and started toward her office.

"Oh, Dr. Hartnett? You got another e-mail from the provost. He really needs those budget-variance documents. He says this is your second deadline."

"Yes, I'm sure he does. Okay, thanks." And the door closed behind her.

Lucy stared at the door for maybe ten seconds. It wasn't like Alexis to be this far behind during budget season. Lucy knew, as surely as she knew her own Social Security number, that the reason had something to do with Dr. Joe Barnes.

ఇ

Joe read the cover letter one more time, then started to scan it again.

*Come on, Barnes! Just put the stupid thing in the mail!*

He slid the vinyl loose-leaf binder into the on-campus envelope. He scribbled through the previous name and mail stop and wrote the number for the dean's office. He looked at it a few seconds, then added "Re: Thomson Faculty Renewal Fellowship Application." Not that Lucy would have any trouble figuring out what she was supposed to do with the packet; having the words on the envelope just made Joe feel better.

He carried the packet down the hall and handed it to the bored-looking student worker in the department's workroom. "Hey, Riki. How's it coming with Dr. Gamble?"

"Oh, not so bad, I guess. I just never knew Shakespeare could be dissected so many different ways."

Joe smiled at her. "Yeah, it's too bad, isn't it? But I think you really will come out on the other side with a deeper appreciation for the music of his language."

"Um, Dr. B....that's exactly one of the phrases she told us she didn't want to hear—ever—in her class. 'An upper-level course is no place to indulge ill-informed adolescent fantasies. We're here to learn how to take things apart and put them together again.'"

Joe raised his eyebrows. "Oops. Didn't mean to hit a sore spot."

"Not your fault, Dr. B. I'll make sure your packet goes out."

"Thanks."

Joe walked back toward his office. He glanced at his watch. Twenty minutes until his Brit Lit class. Enough time to make the adjustments in his lecture notes. Hopefully, a little further explanation of Coleridge's historical context and less-than-idyllic life would alleviate the disturbing pharmaceutical assumptions he'd glimpsed in the last round of essays. Joe thought about his faculty fellowship proposal. Why, after all these years and all that had happened, did he suddenly feel so compelled to delve back into Hawthorne? Too late to worry about that now. The packet was in the mail; the next person to see it would be Lucy, over in Alexis's office.

Alexis...

*No time for that now, Joe. Lecture notes, remember?*

He went into his office and dug through the stacks on his desk until he located the pad with today's class notes. He made arrows and stars at the appropriate points on the typed outline, ran a highlighter over a few places, then began tucking everything into his valise. He was reaching for his dog-eared *Norton Anthology* when one of the memories, pouncing from some unsuspected hiding place, gripped him with a pain as gleaming and hard as a scalpel.

*Her hair, backlit by the full moon...*

Joe dropped the thick paperback into his valise and closed his eyes, leaning forward onto his desk. *It wasn't me; it wasn't the material; it was just a crazy combination of circumstances,* he told himself for the millionth time. *I did the right thing, the only thing I could. The dean of students was compassionate, nobody tried to embarrass anybody, and it was all over and done with. She is probably married, has two or three kids by now, and hasn't thought about me in years. And God knew, no matter what anyone said, the whole business was purely tangential to...all the mess that followed. So just let it go and do your job.*

Joe grabbed the *Norton* and thumbed to the assigned reading for today's class: Blake's "The Lamb" and "The Tyger." He pondered, not for the first time, whether all the rhetoric he would expend in class today, urging the students not to be suckered in by the simple appearance and childish meter of the poems, was really worth the effort. Maybe Blake really did mean nothing more than to evoke a sort of innocent wonder at the prodigal diversity of creation. Maybe Joe's students could do little better than simply revel in juvenile amazement at a world that could simultaneously house the lamb's harmless innocence and the tiger's fearful symmetry.

And then Joe started wondering what other strange beasts prowled the forests of his mind's night. What lurking predator had flushed out the memory that had flown in his face just now?

There was a tap on his doorframe. Joe turned around in his chair.

"Hi. Got a minute?"

It was Sophie Namath. "Sure, Dr. Namath. About that long before my next class, but come on in."

"Oh, I have to go too. I just wanted to drop by and see if you ever got that proposal submitted. And it's 'Sophie,' remember?"

"Oh, sorry. Yeah, I did. And thanks again for the reading."

"No problem; glad to do it. Some fine stuff in there. Good luck with the committee."

"Thanks."

"Which way's your class?"

Joe pointed.

"Me too. Walk with you?"

"Sure, why not?" Joe ran an arm through the shoulder strap on his valise and picked up the *Norton*. "Ready?"

She nodded. Joe pulled the office door shut behind him.

"Where were you before coming here?" Sophie asked. She pulled a mandarin orange out of the side pocket of her cardigan, thrust a long, red-lacquered thumbnail into the navel, and began peeling as they walked.

"New York."

"Really? Which university?"

"None of them. I was working at Harper and Row. Editing."

"You're kidding. You left the glamorous world of publishing to come teach?" She gave him a sideways look as she popped a section of orange into her mouth. "Whatever for?"

He ducked his head and grinned. "Can't tell you now. You'll laugh me out of here."

"Oh, let me guess. You missed the thrill of liberating young minds from thralldom to MySpace and iTunes."

Joe kept grinning. He couldn't look at her.

"Please, spare us," she said. "Orange?"

"No, thanks. Well, you asked."

"Yeah. So how long were you at Harper?"

"Twelve years this last time."

Sophie shook her head. "I don't get it. Working with actual literates, and you chuck it all—"

"You're thinking about Susan Sontag and T. C. Boyle. Most of the people who get edited in the trade houses aren't quite on a par."

"How bad can it be?"

26

"Think about the first draft of an NFL MVP's memoirs."

"Ah."

"And the acquisitions people have paid high six figures for the hardback and paper rights, and the book's in the fall catalog so it can get onto shelves before Thanksgiving, and the, um, author doesn't turn in the manuscript until, oh, say, the second week of training camp."

She grimaced, nodding her head. "Yeah, I get it. And you're the guy who sucks up the time lag."

"Bingo. Needless to say, I didn't get a cut of sales. Just yelled at if the project didn't hit its deadline."

"Sort of makes grading freshman essays sound not so bad."

"Well, the writing quality is pretty similar."

"Here's my stop," she said. She popped the last section of the orange into her mouth and dropped the flayed skin into the trash can just inside the classroom door. She tilted her head back and looked at him. "Couldn't stay away from the classroom, eh? So why'd you leave it in the first place?"

"That's a story for another time."

She nodded. "Well, maybe I'll have to hear it. Say, over a drink?"

He gave her a look that he was sure was a little too surprised. "Oh, uh, yeah. Fine. Whenever. Well…guess I'd better get along."

He walked on, almost certain she was still watching him.

⌖

Lucy tapped on the door, then walked into the dean's office. Alexis looked up.

"Do you still have the fellowship notebook?" Lucy said.

Alexis pointed at the floor beside her desk. Lucy picked up the book and turned to go.

"More applications?"

"Yes. I need to update this."

"Is my three o'clock here yet?"

"No."

"Good. I can use the extra time. These budget variances are killing me."

Lucy closed the door behind her and went to her desk. The on-campus mail was spilled across her credenza, and on top of the heap was an envelope meticulously addressed to Dean Hartnett, with the additional notation "Re: Thomson Faculty Renewal Fellowship Application." As if Lucy wouldn't know from the packet what it was for.

She unwound the cord closure and pulled the binder from the envelope. It fell open to the cover page, and the first words she saw were "A proposal submitted by Dr. Joseph Barnes."

Lucy thumbed through the packet. It was scrupulously prepared, of course; no surprise there. Everything Dr. B. did was perfect.

She could just imagine the flutter in Alexis's heart when this proposal landed on her desk. She'd put aside whatever else she was doing and read the thing from beginning to end. Never mind about the departmental evaluations; never mind about the budget reports; never mind about anything except Joe Barnes.

Lucy shook her head. She'd been around the block a time or two; she knew an opportunist when she saw one. Dr. B. could flash that cute smile all he wanted; Lucy wasn't taken in. Alexis had been hurt enough in her life. Lucy wasn't about to let it happen on her watch.

## THREE

T he grapefruit-sized ball arced through the air and thudded on the turf, bounced heavily twice, then rolled to a stop about a handbreadth from the jack. A moan went up from the history faculty.

"That's rollin' 'em, Al! Make 'em sweat, baby!"

Tielman bent over and did a couple of celebratory fist pumps before walking back to stand beside the other English profs. Fred Govanian palmed his boccie ball and toed the line, sending a malevolent squint toward the ball Al had just expertly placed.

"Nice one, Al," Sophie Namath said. "Grape?"

"What've you got the pockets of that cardigan lined with?" Tielman said, giving the fruit a skeptical look. "I don't really care for fuzz with my snacks." Sophie rolled her eyes and popped a grape into her mouth.

"I can't believe I'm standing on the lawn in front of the administration building, playing boccie," Joe said. "I thought I'd played my last game when I left New York. I think the old men in Central Park were glad to see me go."

"Hey, this isn't just any game," Tielman said. "The Catcher's Cup is at stake. And Govanian's still smarting over the spanking we gave history this time last year."

There was a loud click, followed by a roar from the history faculty. Tielman whirled around. Govanian's toss had knocked Al's ball six or seven feet away and left the history professor closest to the lemon-sized jack. He did a middle-aged white man's imitation of a moonwalk and jabbed his forefingers in Tielman's direction.

"Guess I'm up," Joe said.

"Yeah, put it to 'em, Joey. Send Govanian back to the antebellum period."

Joe walked to the line. He bent over at the waist and made a couple of preparatory swings, then released his ball on a long, low trajectory. It rolled toward Govanian's ball and bumped against it, nudging it about a foot away from the jack. Joe's ball nestled about the length of a forefinger from the yellow target ball.

Al gave a war whoop, and the rest of the English faculty cheered.

"Hey, new guy, what's the big idea?" Fred Govanian had his fists on his hips, glaring at Joe.

"Too bad, Govanian," Tielman said. "Joe here's a ringer we brought in from the big city just to make sure we put it to you guys one more time." Govanian gave a disgusted shake of his head and waved Tielman off.

Somewhere in the back of the English department gallery, a low chant began, then built slowly and steadily: "Catcher's Cup… Catcher's Cup…Catcher's Cup…"

"Hey, come on. This little match isn't over by a long shot," Govanian said. The history faculty rallied behind him with a little good-natured shoving along the boundary between themselves and the English contingent.

The next player for the history department was a drop-dead gorgeous blonde in a Yale T-shirt a shade tighter than professional, in Joe's opinion.

"Who's that?" Joe said to Sophie.

"Dr. Kenton." She laid a careful stress on *Dr.*

"No way she's old enough to have a terminal degree."

"Govanian keeps her around to maintain the department's enrollment numbers."

"And the morale of the male faculty?"

"She's really good in the classroom, they say."

"Which 'they'?"

"Not sure."

Kenton eyed the target zone. Joe's ball was between the foot line and the jack, so if she tried to move his ball away, she risked fouling on the jack. She moved along the line, studying the angles. Joe guessed every male eye in the crowd was moving with her, though not necessarily thinking about the same angles.

Sophie offered Joe a grape, which he declined. She shook her head and gave a wry smile.

"What?" he said.

Sophie pointed with her chin toward Dr. Kenton. "Gwen loves this. You can tell."

"I don't think the men mind it either."

"Why do you think this goofy little match is so well attended?"

"How long has she been on the faculty?"

"Two years."

"Spike in interest a couple of years ago?"

"Oh, please. You could practically smell the testosterone."

Joe snickered softly.

Gwen Kenton had apparently made her decision; she was on the left end of the foot line, readying her shot. She lofted the ball toward the target and hit Joe's ball, knocking it into the jack. Her ball ricocheted away to the right, coming to rest about three feet away. It was unclear to Joe whether his was still closest to the jack.

"Foul!" Tielman said, striding toward the jack. "She touched the jack. Joe's ball goes back where it was."

"Wait a minute, Tielman. Gwen didn't hit the jack. She hit Joe, and he hit the jack. I say the balls stay in play."

"No way, Fred. It wasn't a called shot, so the jack is inviolate, as you well know. Don't make me get the rule book."

"What rule book?"

Some bickering ensued, with both sides generating a good deal more heat than light. In the end, the history department's appeal to tradition carried the day, and Gwen's throw was declared a tie with Joe's position after her toss. Then Al was up again.

"I'm gonna make you wish you never opened your pie hole, Govanian."

"You tell him, Tielman," Sophie said.

Joe looked at her. "Odd. I didn't have you pegged as the partisan type."

She shrugged. "Hey, it's the Catcher's Cup. Brings out the worst."

"Heaven save us. The barbarians are at the gate, and they are us."

"Oh, come on, Dr. Barnes. You're doing your part to egg on the rowdies."

"My department chair asked me to play. I'm just following orders, ma'am."

"That defense didn't work at Nuremberg either."

"Ouch."

She gave him a good-natured slap on the shoulder, and he slipped her a discreet elbow. They laughed.

Joe watched Al sizing up his shot and tried not to think about all the midterm exams on his desk, waiting to be graded. His eyes roved toward the administration building; its neoclassical facade hovered over the contest like a dowager at a church picnic. Alexis's office was somewhere on the third floor, Joe thought—maybe that window there?

The shade was up, and a figure was framed in the window. It was too far for Joe to be certain, but it could easily be Alexis, watching from her Olympian vantage point as the silliness continued below.

He suddenly felt an odd tendril of self-consciousness, standing beside Sophie. Might someone—never mind who—imagine he was flirting with her? Was he? And why did that seem to matter more just these last few seconds?

Alexis watched as Tielman made his pitch. She could hear the sounds of hilarity through her closed window. It looked like Al had put the English team back on the inside. She could see Fred Govanian gesturing and shaking his head as he walked to the line.

The Catcher's Cup. Not so long ago she'd stood on the lawn with the English faculty. It was midterm, wasn't it? The semesters seemed to go round faster these days since she wasn't in the classroom on a regular basis.

It was one of those clear late-autumn days that always made her wish for a long novel and a chair in the sun. As she'd walked from the parking lot this morning, the air held the flat, cool scent of weather poised for a change. Days like this, when they came in late October and November, seemed to her like last call at a favorite pub or the final dance of the prom.

Joe and Sophie seemed to be enjoying themselves. With a bit of concentration, Alexis thought she could probably talk herself out of the little twinge of jealousy she felt as she saw the two of them laughing together.

*Junior high was a long, long time ago, dear. You really ought to move on, don't you think?*

The door opened behind her. Lucy came in and put a bulging folder on her desk. Her eyes flitted toward the window, then to Alexis's face, then away as she left the office and closed the door behind her.

Alexis noted the flash of embarrassment—quickly followed by annoyance—instigated by Lucy's entrance. Why should Lucy care if her boss was looking out the window on a beautiful Indian summer day? And why did Alexis feel so defensive about it?

*Why do I keep asking myself questions and then refusing the answers?*

She looked out the window even while feeling the drag of the folder—its dry, silent, papery clamor pulling her toward her desk. For a few more seconds she yearned for the lawn, the day, the sheltering vastness of the golden afternoon. Then she went to her desk and picked up the file.

*❦*

"You really learned to play boccie in Central Park?" Sophie said.

Joe nodded, sliding his mug around in tiny circles on its cardboard coaster. "You think the Catcher's Cup is intense? Wait till you're the deciding pitch in a game between a team of old Italian men and a bunch of geezers from Warsaw."

"Which team were you on?"

He shrugged. "Whichever one had the best pastries that day."

She laughed. "An opportunist to the core, then."

"I don't mess around when there's fresh, home-baked babka on the line."

"So what's your story, Dr. B.?" Sophie propped her cheek in her palm, stirred her drink, and looked at him with a tilted expression.

"What do you mean?"

"Just that you don't add up, that's all. You're hiding something is my guess."

Joe gave her what he hoped looked like a careless roll of the eyes. He tipped his mug and took a sip. He looked around the crowded watering hole.

Uncle Thursday's was like a thousand bar-and-grill joints across from a thousand college campuses. Everything from the carefully haphazard arrangement of the antique sporting equipment on the walls to the faux Tiffany lamps suspended from the ceiling around the bar—it all had the generic ring of familiarity. The frats congregated in the corner farthest from the door, while the few faculty who had nothing better to do during happy hour tended to cluster in the booths along the front wall.

His eyes returned to Sophie; she was studying him with a coquettish half smile.

"What?"

"You're not going to tell, are you?"

"Nope. I intend to remain an enigma, inside a mystery, wrapped in a puzzle."

"Churchill is rolling over in his grave."

"And I'm rolling home." He clunked his mug onto the table and stood up.

"Touchy, touchy! Must be an exposed nerve."

"That or a stack of midterms to grade. See you tomorrow, Sophie."

"I make you uncomfortable. Is that it?"

He looked down at her. She still wore that amused, curious expression that was hard to ignore and equally hard to dislike.

"Yeah, you saw through me, Sofe. I have a pathological fear of persons who share a family name with former AFL quarterbacks. Something about an incident in gym class that was so humiliating I've buried the memory deep in my subconscious."

"No relation. At least I never saw him at any family reunions."

"What a relief. Our budding relationship lives to fight another day. So…can I go now?"

She shrugged and took another sip of her drink. "Sure. I got all the time in the world. Nice playing with you."

He made a face at her while he fished a dollar from his wallet. "For the waitperson," he said, allowing the bill to flutter to a resting place beside his half-empty mug. He pointed at her, then wiggled good-bye with his fingers. She gave him a parting salute with her glass.

He opened the door, then ducked backward, narrowly avoiding being bowled over by a skateboarder careening down the sidewalk. "Sorry, man," the kid tossed over his shoulder.

Joe just hiked the strap of his valise back onto his shoulder and walked toward his car.

Why did it seem that, despite his best efforts to be unassuming, his colleagues were intent on ferreting out his past? He remembered Al Tielman's abortive quizzing at his apartment, and now Sophie Namath had apparently adopted as her goal the complete unveiling of all the deep, dark secrets she imagined in his past. It went beyond the good-natured probing that was a part of building an acquaintance; Sophie gave full evidence of being on a mission.

Would it be so unpleasant to be the object of her attentions? She was bright, witty, extremely competent, and completely unattached. Why shouldn't professional peers date if they felt like it?

Maybe that was it; maybe he didn't feel like it.

Across the street from Uncle Thursday's was a park. Elms and maples rose like pillars from the turf, and beneath them were concrete benches and meandering walkways. It would have been an idyllic setting, but the skaters had taken possession of the space. The boy who had almost collided with him was taking slow, looping runs at one of the benches, then leaping into the air in an attempt to perform some unfathomable maneuver that involved scraping his skateboard across the bench. The air was full of the sound of neoprene wheels on concrete, of the slapping of the boards against various obstacles, and the grunts of the skaters as they became momentarily airborne. They stood about in clumps, watching impassively as each took a run at a bench or a set of steps or a stair railing. Joe couldn't tell what differentiated success from failure; each skater's attempt was greeted by the same passive observation. In their collective silence and apparent unity of purpose, they might have been a society of telepaths in baggy clothing and toboggan caps.

It was often difficult to distinguish between success and failure, Joe thought. To the outsider, much of the academic enterprise was likely as incomprehensible as a gathering of skateboarders. Joe tried to imagine his father, a retired over-the-road trucker and lifelong member of the Teamsters Union, sitting in on one of his son's presentations at a literary conference. Or his mother, a typical wife and mother of the fifties—what would she make of, say, the last article he'd published, a comparative analysis of the functional vocabularies of William Faulkner and William Shakespeare? Wouldn't it all seem to them much like the kids across the street seemed to him: lots of standing around, a little thrashing and grunting, then more standing? At least the skateboarders were getting some exercise and fresh air.

Joe thought about the midterm exams that would occupy his evening. Most would be barely more than dreadful; a few would be cogent enough to be tolerable. For most of his students, Joe's class was an obstacle to be overcome on the way to a degree in accounting or fashion merchandising or elementary education.

But a handful would show flashes of original thought. For a few gifted students, the lure of language would prove too much to resist. They would move on into the upper-level courses, then into graduate studies, then into doctoral programs, then out into the exotic world of literary conferences and journal articles on arcane topics. All to earn the right to stand in front of a classroom of students and inspire three or four percent of them to learn, in their turn, how to spawn more makers of erudite minutiae.

Joe sometimes wondered how academia escaped the law of diminishing returns. If scholars continued to learn more and more about less and less, how much longer could it be until everything was known about nothing?

*Don't go there, Joe. That way lies madness...*

With such a healthy store of cynicism, was it any wonder he found it hard to accept Sophie Namath's interest at face value?

# FOUR

L ucy was in a sour mood, a kind of low-hanging, hovering
malaise that was all the more annoying because she couldn't
put her finger on its origin. She felt this way every year just after the
income-tax-filing deadline, worrying that she'd forgotten something
that would come back to bite her in the rear. Or for the first twelve
hours after she'd left on vacation when she couldn't escape the nig-
gling sensation that the coffeepot was still on, or she'd forgotten to
have her mail held.

So far, none of her dire half premonitions had come to pass, but
that didn't keep her from running a mental and emotional checklist
every so often—a sort of internal scouting report. You couldn't be too
careful. At least Lucy didn't think so.

She hit Save on the spreadsheet she was creating for Alexis and
reached into the drawer in her desk that held her purse. She removed
her well-worn, brown leather planner from the side pocket and flipped
through the calendar to November. She scanned the coming week.

Polly's birthday fell on the third Wednesday this year, the week before Thanksgiving. Good. She hadn't forgotten. It would've just killed her to fail to get Polly's card in the mail in plenty of time. But she hadn't, so that couldn't be what was nagging at her. She jotted "Polly—card" on a sticky note and thumbed it to the edge of her computer screen. She'd go by the campus store during her lunch break and pick out one of the funny cards Polly liked so much. Maybe one of those new square ones that required extra postage.

Lucy wished her brother took a little more notice of Polly. She was such a sweet girl—far and away Lucy's favorite of her nephews and nieces. Polly had stayed with her a few summers back, and they'd had such a good time. Polly was a bright one too; she'd likely graduate with honors from Stanford next May. She had every reason to be proud and confident.

Which made what had happened all the worse. That sorry excuse for a professor. He should've been fired, or worse. "I know it was wrong, but I couldn't help myself," he'd said. Lucy could've helped him, all right—helped him out of a job and maybe more than that. Poor Polly. Such a sweet girl, so innocent. And those crocodile tears of his...

Lucy went back to the spreadsheet. She highlighted the last column, then clicked Total. She looked at the number that appeared at the bottom. She bit her lip and shook her head. Alexis wasn't going to like this. Nor, for that matter, would the provost.

Alexis had been under such pressure lately. From what Lucy could tell, the infighting over the budget was worse than usual this year. Not that any college in the country would ever announce that it was rolling in funds, but every time Alexis came back from a meeting with the provost or the finance committee, Lucy wound up having to do a report or a spreadsheet that drew the funding circle smaller and smaller. Like any good leader, Alexis was fighting for her organization, trying to keep the budget cutters looking somewhere other than her college for the reductions needed to make the bottom line balance. But it was getting harder and harder. The cuts were coming, and nothing Alexis or any of the other deans could do appeared to be changing that fact.

Lucy straightened up the spreadsheet columns and put the headings in bold type. She formatted the background color of the rows in alternating gray and white, the way Alexis preferred. She saved it a final time, then sent it to her printer. Alexis had asked to see it as soon as it was finished.

Maybe she'd actually be concentrating on work when Lucy went in instead of watching some silly interdepartmental game. Lucy shook her head as she waited for the spreadsheet to queue up on her printer. She hadn't missed the guilty look that flashed across Alexis's face. Lucy didn't even need to look to know that Dr. B. was right in the middle of the goofy mob out on the lawn; she could see it in Alexis's blush.

Well, Lucy made sure his application was buried deep in the stack. Alexis would find it, certainly, but before she did, she'd have to know how many applications were ahead of his, applications from faculty with far more seniority.

Lucy wondered briefly why she'd bothered. Alexis hardly needed her administrative assistant's approval to assign or withdraw funding. Of course, there was always the committee to consider, but Alexis could tip things heavily by appearing to sponsor or have doubts about one of the applicants.

The printer began to whir. With a flash of frustration, Lucy realized she'd forgotten to format the document for one page per sheet; she'd have to redo it and print it again. She tugged the sheets from the printer tray and tossed them into the recycling bag, then clicked through the formatting options. Even she was losing focus, Lucy realized. Not good. Somebody in this office needed to be minding the store. It was up to her.

❧

The provost stared at the report, then laid it facedown atop the stack of similar proposals. He bridged his fingertips and made a sideways, chin-jerking motion that told Alexis his collar was chafing his neck.

"Dr. Hartnett, I appreciate the position you're in, but you have to appreciate mine."

*Appreciate.* It was one of Clement's favorite words. *We need to do more to appreciate the concerns of all our stakeholders at this university… Until due appreciation has been given to the allegations made by the NCAA, the university can't comment on any actions being contemplated…*

"Phil, we've been over this before. I've already got people teaching overloads in three of my departments. The accreditation people did enough finger wagging on their most recent visit to last me for—"

"Dr. Hartnett, I can appreciate—"

"Phil, you're not listening to me."

The provost sat back in his chair and blinked at her. Phil Clement always reminded her less of an educator than a bank president from the 1890s. With a center part and some pince-nez, he'd have been William Howard Taft.

"I've trimmed fat, but now you're asking me to cut into the muscle. How many lecture classes of fifty or a hundred students can we offer before we start undermining the reason these kids come here in the first place? At some point it has to come down to one teacher connecting with one student in a way that makes a difference. My college can't do that in a mass-instruction setting. Sure, my student loads look funny; in the College of Arts and Humanities we have music teachers giving private lessons to one student at a time. We have graduate-level history majors doing individual guided studies. We have highly specialized areas where the upper-level classes are always going to be small. And these happen to be accreditation requirements. What about athletics, Phil? Is Larry DeWitt going to have to take responsibility for the defensive line in addition to being head coach? Somehow I doubt it. Come on, Phil, you're killing me here."

*Careful, old girl. You're rapidly approaching the border between "strong and direct" and the Land of the B Word. Best to begin decelerating...*

Clement stared at her for a few seconds. He looked away, drumming his fingertips on the table.

"Alexis, please try to remember that we're on the same team here. You and I both want what's best for this university and its students and faculty; you must believe that."

Alexis took a slow breath and let it drain. "Yes, Dr. Clement. Of course I believe that."

"And you must also believe that the financial realities of our current situation sit just as heavily on me as they do on you."

Briefly Alexis wondered if the two assistant provosts Clement had hired in the last five years were worrying whether their positions would be funded next year. She nodded.

"Well, then." Phil Clement picked up the reports and stacked them, then laid them in front of him again. "I trust you'll understand how best to proceed. Was there anything else?"

Alexis had her eyes closed. She shook her head.

"Fine." He glanced at his watch. "I think Dr. Kelcy should be waiting outside. Please send him in."

Alexis pushed herself up from the table and went into the outer office. Richard Kelcy was indeed perched on the edge of a green vinyl armchair just outside the door. He looked up at her with a question on his face. Alexis shook her head.

Dr. Kelcy took a deep breath. He gripped his briefcase and stood, waiting for her to pass.

"Good luck, Richard. Hope you score more points than I did."

She went out. Kelcy was dean of the College of Science and Mathematics. He had lots of professors writing lots of research grants for projects that used one or two student assistants. Alexis wondered how his student loads would look on Clement's graphs.

The provost's office was on the same floor as Alexis's; the halls were lined with faded portraits of past administrators or patrons of the school. Outside a few of the office doors bulletin boards were tacked haphazardly with announcements, memos, and notices of furniture or computers for sale, most with convenient tear-off strips across the bottom containing the seller's phone number. The gaps from the torn-off strips gave the notices a tattered, unzipped look. Alexis guessed maybe five or six hundred students and staffers walked past these bulletin boards every day. Some of the notices, forgotten or expired, had grown brittle with age.

Last night Alexis had dreamed she was in the house of some friends when the doorbell rang. Through the window she could see one of the elders of her church standing on the doorstep. When the door opened, he started firing some kind of automatic weapon. She dropped down between a couch and the wall, and he stepped into the room, making sure everyone was dead. He went outside, and she could see someone bringing what appeared to be an explosive device toward the house. She had never actually seen an explosive device firsthand, but in the kaleidoscopic logic of her dream, the device was clearly a bomb.

She started crawling toward the back of the house, and somehow the walls and ceiling lifted up, like someone taking the lid off a cardboard box. Apparently, the universe was conspiring to flush her out of hiding. She crawled off the back steps of the house and was on some kind of large, flat go-cart. The engine started, and she was barreling backward down the alley just as the house exploded in a ball of orange flame.

The next thing she knew, she was in a salt cave so vast that it had its own sky and mountain ranges. Chambers were cut into the salt, and people hid in them—from what, it didn't occur to her dreaming mind to wonder. Some of the rooms had religious imagery carved into the salt: icons of saints, crosses, words in ancient-looking Greek. One of the rooms had what appeared to be a baptistery sunk into the salt floor.

Alexis awoke from the dream and stared at the dark ceiling of her bedroom. It was some time before she could go back to sleep.

What gave dreams their power? Sometimes the more outlandish and unbelievable they were, the more they haunted her, puzzled her. What was going into her subconscious at this moment that might arise tonight in some twisted, Rorschachian apparition to stalk her sleep?

She had plenty of memories that could keep her awake without the need for distracting, surreal imagery. Her marriage to Brooks, for example. There were enough snarled communications, enough hurts inflicted despite the best of intentions to busy a team of Freudian archaeologists for a good six months. It had been almost a year since she'd had any contact with Brooks. But with the children grown and moved on, there wasn't any good excuse for contact. She'd heard he was working on another history of the Merovingian dynasty. She'd also heard that his young postdoctoral companion had moved on. She felt vaguely sorry for him—but not surprised.

When she taught English, Alexis used to tell her students to try to understand the assumptions behind the words—those of the masters they read and their own as they wrote their compositions. She wanted them at least to try to glimpse the architecture of meaning. Of course, that was before the deconstructionists started building their hegemony. Nowadays, apparently you could say an igloo was a Gothic cathedral as long as you constructed an adroit syllogism.

But the way it all fit together, the logic of it—that was what mystified Alexis. She wanted to get her arms around it. She wanted to discover the Rosetta stone, the unified field theory of consciousness. Alexis suffered from the belief that if she could just grasp the "it" at the center of everything, the mismatched puzzle pieces of her life would fall into place. The path to enlightenment would lie open before her.

And maybe she could even get her budget approved. That, and quit toying with distracting ideas about…certain faculty members.

# FIVE

L ucy glanced at the clock. Eleven thirty-five. If she planned to have any time for lunch, she had to get these last packets ready for the fellowship committee meeting that was supposed to start at one. Everything was done except for clipping the applicant's CV on the outside of each packet.

She slid the paper clip over the last packet, then realized it was Joe Barnes's. She stared at it for a few seconds, wishing she could think of some way to lose it before reaching the committee meeting room. Then she noticed something. She couldn't understand why she'd never noticed it before.

There was a twelve-year gap in his teaching experience.

His time in the editorial department at Harper and Row was noted, of course, so it wasn't like there was a mysterious hiatus in his employment history. But to be out of teaching for twelve years... Something about it didn't feel right.

And what was his rank when he left his previous university? He ought to at least have made associate professor, but there was no notation on his résumé. Very odd. Unless…he was trying to conceal something.

She stared at the CV a few more seconds, then, with a quick glance at the door, slid the document from beneath its clip and carried it to the copy machine. She made a copy, then put the original back in its place. She folded the copy and put it in the lap drawer of her desk.

Lucy gathered the fellowship packets in a double armload and started down the hallway to the dean's conference room. She would place them in a stack at the head of the table, and Alexis would pass them around to the committee, giving a thumbnail sketch of each applicant and his or her proposed project to be funded by the fellowship stipend. There would be subsequent meetings, and some of the applicants would be invited to make a fuller presentation to the committee.

But before this process got very far along, Lucy decided, she would know more about Joe Barnes's twelve-year absence from the classroom.

*✑*

Joe squeezed the handles of the garlic press. The extruded garlic made a satisfying crackle as it fell into the hot olive oil. He dumped in the chopped onion and bell pepper and stirred. He glanced at the chicken breast baking in the toaster oven. Looked like it was browning nicely.

The garlic toast! The bread was still in the cabinet, unbuttered. Joe shook his head. Too late now; everything else was almost ready. He always forgot something. He took a swallow of Shiraz and swirled it in his mouth, dabbing now and again at the vegetables in the sauté pan.

His doorbell rang. He set the wineglass on the counter and went to the door and peered through the pane. It was Sophie. *What on earth...*

He opened the door.

"Hi, stranger. You've been making yourself scarce around the department these last few days. I came by to see if you'd died in your easy chair or something."

He let the door fall open, and she breezed past him, removing her coat and tossing it across the back of his couch.

"No easy chair, I see. Well, that's a relief anyway. Mmm, something smells good. Am I in time for dinner?"

He still stood at the doorway, arms akimbo, shaking his head. "Sure, if you don't mind sharing a rather small chicken breast."

"No, thanks, dear. Actually I ate before I came over. Usually best, I've found, when making unexpected house calls on bachelors."

"Well, there's no teacher like experience."

She stuck out her tongue at him. "I would love a glass of whatever you're drinking though."

"By all means." He went to the cabinet, retrieved a glass, and poured it half-full of Shiraz. "I assume there's some explanation forthcoming about the reason for this surprising, delightful, and completely unannounced visit?"

She held the glass to her nose and inhaled deeply, keeping her eyes on his. "Mulberry, spice, and...maybe a hint of plum?"

Joe shrugged. "It all smells like fermented grape juice to me."

"Philistine." She took a swallow, then gestured with her glass toward the kitchen. "Please, don't let your supper burn. Where's your bathroom?"

"Through there. Make yourself at home." He turned away as he said it, so she couldn't see the grimace. It wasn't that he was inhospitable; he just didn't feel entirely comfortable playing impromptu host to someone as mercurial as Sophie. That anyone—possibly including Sophie—could predict what errand she was on, he seriously questioned.

When she came out, he was sliding the vegetables onto a plate beside the sizzling chicken breast. He waved at one of the stools lined up on the other side of the counter. "Have a seat. Drink your wine. And please tell me...whatever it is you intended to tell me."

She came around the counter, stood directly in front of him, and kissed him—a lingering, undulating kiss with worlds of intent behind it. She pulled away. Joe realized his eyes probably looked like headlights on high beam. Sophie started giggling.

"Well, you certainly make up in intensity what you lack in vocabulary," he said.

"Yeah, well, I like the direct approach." She leaned toward him again, but he backed away.

"Sophie, wait a minute. This…isn't going to work."

She tilted her head and gave him a questioning look. "What isn't?"

"I mean… Sophie, you don't just walk in and—"

"Why not?"

He stared at her. Was this some ploy of hers, some strategy to excavate his past? Emotional electroshock therapy? Well, he wasn't interested.

"Listen, Sophie. You're great to be with—and I probably ought to have my head examined—but I really need to ask you to back off."

She tucked her hands under her arms and studied him as though she thought, but wasn't quite sure, she'd just been insulted.

"You sure it's your head you need examined?"

"Sophie, now don't take this the wrong way—"

"What's the right way, Joe?"

"C'mon now. Not every man is looking for a quick roll in the sack, just like not every woman's looking for Mr. Commitment."

"These are the options then?"

"You know what I mean."

"I'm not sure I do." She looked at him for several seconds, and there wasn't a smile lurking anywhere on her face. "Well, guess I figured you all wrong. Sorry." She went to the couch and began pulling on her coat. "See you around."

And she was gone.

Joe stared at the closed door for maybe a full thirty seconds. He took a deep breath and closed his eyes. Her wineglass still sat on the counter, now one swallow less than half-full. The wrinkled crescent of her lip was still printed in pale pink highlights on the rim. Joe picked up the glass, gave the Shiraz a last, longing look, and poured it down the drain. He rinsed the glass and set it beside the sink.

He ate his dinner with elbows on the counter, slouched over his plate like some derelict sitting in a soup kitchen. He thought briefly about putting on some music, but the effort of going to the CD rack and actually making a decision seemed too much. Sophie had launched a frontal assault on his self-restraint; she'd performed an unauthorized experiment with his psychosexual response system. So why did he feel like the guilty one?

Sophie was an attractive colleague. She was a fine teacher. She was...pretty direct, as she said, but that wasn't always bad, was it? There were probably plenty of men who'd have taken her invitation as far as she'd have allowed and been glad of the chance. And if he were brutally honest with himself, he'd have to admit he wasn't completely displeased by the opportunity.

*What, then?*

Joe thought about Carol, about the last few years of their marriage. How he'd wished there was some way past the detritus of all the unintentional wounds and scars they left behind. After a while it wasn't even about the hurts themselves, anymore, the list of grievances; it was about the whole system, the whole intimate accumulation of regret and guilt and dull, unyielding anger. The sheer bulk of it became too much somehow. Their marriage fell apart under its own weight. At first when it was all over, he'd been unable to feel much of anything except relief.

And then he began to realize that he was lonely. And that scared him. It undermined the bitter comfort of having the divorce as an excuse.

None of which precisely explained why he couldn't let himself take a chance on Sophie.

Tomorrow he'd go to work, and she'd be there. He tried to imagine the heft of the space between them when they saw each other. What would her face show? What would his? There would be an elephant in the room, but maybe he and Sophie would pretend it was an armchair.

The voices stopped just as he walked into the faculty commons. Sophie Namath and Bill Schuman sat at the table in the center of the room, looking at him.

"Morning, troops," Joe said, taking a mug out of the cabinet above the coffee maker. "Planning strategies for today's battles?"

"Trying to figure out who's going to be drummed out of the corps, more like," Sophie said. Joe was relieved to hear her usual half-mocking tone. She'd either forgiven him for last night or decided to fake it.

"What do you mean?"

"Westfield, over in math. He told me there are some big cuts coming down," Schuman said. "Figures. Just when I was about to make assistant professor."

"Come on, Bill," Sophie said. "You know private industry's dying to get their hands on you. You don't need this teaching gig."

"Yeah. No hotter ticket right now than a specialty in Old English and Anglo-Saxon literature," Schuman said.

"It can't be that bad, can it? I haven't heard Al say anything," Joe said.

"Anything about what?" Al Tielman said, walking in.

"Poor Bill is worrying about his job again," Sophie said, patting Schuman on the shoulder. "Be a good department chair, Al. Be reassuring."

"Oh, yeah, I forgot… You're fired, Bill. Hand me a mug, Joe?"

"Very funny." Schuman took a sip of his coffee.

"I don't know what you people are worried about," Tielman said. "The English department's stock has never been higher. I've seen Dr. Hartnett over here more this semester than the last two combined. Besides, Joe here is our talisman."

Joe gave him a surprised look.

"Sure. You helped us win the Catcher's Cup, remember?"

"Oh. I had no idea boccie was so important to the academic enterprise," Joe said.

"How did you think they decide who they're going to downsize?" Schuman said.

"I always assumed it was paper, rock, scissors," Sophie said.

"Well, friends, I'd love to stay and chat, but course evaluations beckon," Tielman said.

"Tell 'em I said hi," Sophie said.

Tielman went out.

"Joe, did you ever hear anything on your renewal-leave proposal?" Schuman said.

"Nope, not yet. From what I understand, the committee only saw the proposals last Thursday."

"Yeah, well, I think you have a really good chance."

"Thanks, Bill."

"They'll probably give you all my classes. Trim the dead wood; let the new hotshot have a clear track."

"I wouldn't doubt it, Bill," Sophie said. "I hear Dr. Hartnett is grooming him for something special."

Joe shot her a look, but her face was averted.

"Well, I'm getting out of here before the encouragement gets any more lethal," Schuman said. He pushed himself up from the table, slouched over to the sink, dumped the remains of his coffee, and rinsed out his mug. "Bye, kids." And he was gone.

Sophie was looking at Joe now. He watched her and waited, trying to guess how the next few minutes would play out.

"I think I've figured something out," she said finally.

"What's that?"

"There really is something about you. More than what's on the surface."

"Well, that's a relief anyway."

"For your information, I'm trying to be nice. Go with me, okay?"

"Sorry." He stood with his hands clasped in front of him, a chastened schoolboy.

"I thought you were just trying to be the mysterious new guy," Sophie said. "Man of shadows, bravely hiding his wounds and forging cheerily ahead into the next phase of his life."

"Interesting mix of attributes."

"Sort of like if Pollyanna had a baby with John Wayne."

"I must admit, you have me pegged."

"Yeah, not so much, you're right. But it was an intriguing hypothesis."

"But on the basis of last night's little experiment…"

"I'm getting to that; don't rush me."

"Sorry again."

"Anyhow, I was determined to penetrate your facade. I thought I could draw you out with charm, and if that didn't work, then animal magnetism would do the trick."

"Ah."

"But I underestimated you."

Joe shrugged. "So what's your next move?"

"Not sure."

"You really think I'm worth the trouble? I can promise you, any slight mystery you might unveil doesn't justify all this effort."

She smiled at him. She pulled an apricot out of the side pocket of her cardigan and took a slurping bite. "Everybody's got to have a hobby." She winked at him.

"Well, all righty then." He swallowed the last of his coffee and turned to rinse his mug.

"Have a good one, Dr. Barnes."

"You, too, Sofe."

"I'll be watching."

He gave her a look over his shoulder. "Somehow I don't doubt that."

## SIX

A lexis could see what was going to happen.

The quantities were known, and the direction of probability was set. Events were converging like lines on a sheet of graph paper. Standing at the zero point was…Joe. There was so little drama in it that she'd have found it completely tedious if it weren't for the inconvenient fact that she cared intensely about what happened to him. Alexis had already decided to mount a delaying action as long as she could. Still, the budget spreadsheets were implacable.

She knew the real drama would begin at the point the consequences came into the open for all to see. What would he do when the crucial realization hit him? She longed with everything in her to know the answer, and at the same time she feared knowing. She was caught in a game she couldn't afford to lose, but she also couldn't leave the table.

Joe's proposal had made the first cut; she never doubted that it would. The committee was unanimous, and she was secretly so proud.

She could hardly wait to give the list to Lucy so she could send out the memos to those whom the committee would interview for the second round. She almost called Joe herself, but that would've been unprofessional at best. Besides, with Lucy watching over her shoulder every minute…

Alexis looked up through her open doorway and saw Joe walk into the reception area. He approached Lucy's desk and pointed with a questioning look at Alexis's door. He got some sort of clipped reply from Lucy and turned toward the door. He saw Alexis at her desk and smiled. Alexis resisted the urge to duck her head like a junior-high kid. Instead, she smiled back.

"Good morning, Dr. Hartnett. I just wanted to say thanks, again, for encouraging me to submit for the fellowship."

"Joe, I don't think we have to stand on ceremony, do we? 'Alexis' will do just fine."

"All right then…Alexis."

"I'm very pleased you put in a proposal, and the committee was favorably impressed. I'm not at all surprised you made the second round."

"Well, thanks. You never know. I'm kind of the low guy on the totem pole around here."

"Please, won't you sit?"

He glanced at his watch. "Yes, sure, I guess there's time. I mean… yeah, I'd like that."

A few seconds passed.

"So, Joe, I'd be interested in your impressions of the English department. You've just come in, as you say. What do you think as a relative outsider?"

He picked at his cuffs. "I think the people are topnotch. They really care about the students, as far as I can see, and they're fine scholars and instructors. There's great collegiality among the faculty for the most part—"

"The deconstructionists."

He gave her a guilty grin. "Well, yeah. But even they're cordial—usually."

"It could be worse." She smiled at him, and despite her best attempts at caution, her eyes got caught in his.

"So." He looked at his watch again. "The committee meets in about ten minutes, right?"

"Ah, yes. They'll have some questions, maybe about your proposed line of study, maybe about your concept of the subject matter, maybe about your methodology—whatever. Anything's fair game."

"Sure. Um, what did you think? Personally?"

"Me? About your proposal?"

He nodded.

"Well, it's… Of course, you realize, I taught English here before going into administration."

"I thought I remembered that. What was your specialty?"

"The transcendentalists, in particular. My dissertation was on Emerson."

"Oops. So you flushed out all the canards in my work in a big hurry, I guess."

She laughed and shook her head. "On the contrary. I find your proposal quite…fascinating. I'm anxious to hear about your final conclusions."

He nodded, and their eyes met again, and now it was Alexis's turn to check the time.

"Well, as you say…"

"Oh, sure." He gathered his portfolio and stood. He made a sweeping gesture toward the door. "Shall we?"

"Thank you."

She walked past him and caught the merest whiff of his after-shave: a spicy, clean scent that made her think of sunny afternoons spent reading on a balcony. She told Lucy they were off to the Thomson fellowship committee meeting in the dean's conference room. And she didn't care what Lucy thought.

❧

The conference room was one of those places that gave evidence of having been built around its furniture. A long mahogany table with a glass top crouched in the center of the room, attended by a dozen hunter green, faux-leather executive chairs. Meeting attendees barely had room between the table and the dark, cherry-paneled wall to roll one of the chairs back far enough to get in or out. Alexis despised the color of the chairs and, for that matter, the whole old-boys'-club feel of the room, but soon after her appointment as dean, she had surmised that this battle wasn't one she was willing to fight. The room and its furnishings had survived maybe three or four deans. As far as Alexis was concerned, her name could be added to the list. It would be the first female name; that was worth something, at least.

"Where does the accused sit?" Joe said.

"Down there, under the spotlights."

He moved toward the end of the table, and she laughed, waving him off. "Just kidding, Joe. Anywhere you like."

He picked a spot about halfway down the table on her right. Alexis, as was her custom, took the place at the end of the table nearest the door. As Joe began pulling his notes from his portfolio, the committee started drifting in.

There was the provost, of course. Phil Clement bumped his way around the table, shifting his bulk this way and that until he was settled in one of the chairs across the table from Joe. The chair complained loudly as Clement leaned back and assumed an expansive expression.

"Afternoon, Dr. Hartnett, Dr. Barnes," he said, nodding to each of them in turn. "Good to see you, Joe. I'm looking forward to hearing more about your proposal."

As Joe exchanged pleasantries with the provost, the chair of the Department of History entered. Fred Govanian glared at Joe as he moved toward the end of the table opposite Alexis. "This is the guy who robbed us of the Catcher's Cup again this year," he said. "His proposal better be good."

Joe held up his hands in mock surrender. "Dr. Govanian, I assure you, my participation in the contest was rendered only under the coercion of my department chair."

"Is Govanian still bellyaching about that thrashing we gave him?" Al Tielman said, standing in the doorway. "Don't worry, Joe; I'll settle his hash. A little more of his lip and I'll tell our guys to take the gloves off next year."

There was some more good-natured ribbing and handshaking, accompanied by the arrival of the chairs of the art, music, and theater departments. When everyone was settled, Alexis called the meeting to order.

"Thank you all for coming. Dr. Thurmond notified me she'd be unable to attend today, but we still have more than a quorum, I believe."

"What's Teresa's excuse this time?" Govanian said. "What's she doing, trying to schedule a new section of second-year Basque so she can wangle another foreign-language instructor?"

"Yeah, she got the idea from that guided study of pre-Columbian Mexico you sneaked into the catalog last fall," Tielman said.

"Hey, Dr. Kenton's specialty is Latin American history!"

"And I'll bet you volunteered to accompany her on all the field trips."

"Um, boys. If we can return to the business at hand," Alexis said.

Phil Clement tsked loudly at the two combatants and shook his head. Govanian muttered something that sounded like "den mother."

"Dr. Barnes's proposal was unanimously approved for the second round, as you know," Alexis said. "I hope you've all had a chance to review his abstract. He's here today to answer any questions you may have about his proposed study. Anybody care to open?"

There was a silence, punctuated by the shuffling of papers and file folders.

"Dr. Barnes has jumped right into the middle of things in our department," Al Tielman said. "He's doing a great job. We're lucky to have him."

There was another long lull.

"Yes, Dr. Barnes, you did your dissertation on Hawthorne, if I remember correctly." Janet Gorman, chair of the art department, peered over her half-lens reading glasses.

"That's correct."

She nodded. "And what is it you want to do with this study that you didn't already cover?"

"Well, Dr. Gorman, in my dissertation I focused more on the mechanics of Hawthorne's style as a function of his place, his era, and the context of American writing at that time in history. With this project, I hope to delve more into the why of his body of work rather than the how."

"What do you think your chances are of getting something published?" Govanian asked.

"Hard to say, Dr. Govanian. Of course, there are a number of journals I've successfully submitted to in the past. A book is harder to place, but we can certainly hope."

"Oh, with all your contacts in New York, you're a shoo-in," Tielman said.

Joe grinned and gave a noncommittal shrug.

"Dr. Barnes, it's a fine proposal, certainly," Clement said, "but I wonder: hasn't Hawthorne kind of been done to death? I mean, what's really different about the direction you plan to take that hasn't already been explored?"

"Fair question, Dr. Clement. Certainly, Hawthorne has been a staple of literary criticism, practically since his first stories were published. But—"

"See, that's what I'm asking. Is there really wisdom in trying to mine a vein that's been worked so much?" He looked around the table at the other committee members. "Shouldn't we concentrate on some line of inquiry that's a little more, well, original?"

There was an awkward silence. Alexis felt her cheeks burning with embarrassment. She'd never heard the provost say more than ten words in a row during one of these meetings. Why the sudden negative interest in Joe's proposal? What was Phil doing?

"Dr. Clement, surely you know that the scholarly enterprise is always subject to peer review and ongoing criticism and countercriticism. That's how it works. Just because a topic's been covered once is no sign it shouldn't be revisited with a different or even contrary emphasis."

Now they were all looking at her—except for Joe. He was staring at his notes, his cheeks tinged with red. Had she really sounded so much like a mother hen? But she was right! Phil Clement had no right to bully Joe in front of the committee.

The provost leaned back in his chair. "Well, Dr. Barnes, maybe your dean has a point. I'm just asking questions here. What do you think? What've you got that's new to toss into the mix?"

Joe shuffled his notes and cleared his throat. "Well, of course, the committee ultimately has to decide on the merits of my proposal. And, as...has already been said, there is often virtue in reexamining familiar material..."

It was painful to watch. Joe was clearly on the defensive. The damage was done. Clement had single-handedly shifted the momentum. But why? Joe said a few more things, and Al Tielman gamely tried to steer the discussion back in a positive direction, but the provost's obvious skepticism hung like a shroud over the rest of the proceedings.

Alexis glanced at her watch. It was time for the next interview.

"Well, thank you, Dr. Barnes. I'm afraid that's all the time we have. Dr. Kenton is probably waiting."

He folded his notes. His face reminded her of someone sitting at a funeral. He aimed a weak smile around the table. "Thanks, everybody." There were murmurs of acknowledgment, but the committee members were shuffling their folders. Nobody except Alexis watched him leave.

# SEVEN

Alexis could barely keep her mind on Gwen Kenton's presentation, which, compared to Joe's, was a love feast. Phil Clement couldn't say enough complimentary things about her research, her skill in the classroom, his interest in her proposed topic. It was almost embarrassing. Even Fred Govanian, her department chair, wore a half-guilty expression. When it was over, Gwen stacked her papers and left, looking as though she'd just put a hotel on Park Place and still had money in the bank.

Clement tried to leave right behind Gwen, but Alexis stood in front of him. "Dr. Clement, could I have a moment please?"

He gave a doubtful glance at his wristwatch. "Well, I have another meeting—"

"Just two minutes?"

The other committee members slipped out the door. Govanian was the last to leave. He gave her an apologetic look as he went out.

Alexis closed the door behind Fred Govanian and turned to face the provost. "Phil, may I ask what in the name of conscience you were doing in here today?"

He actually looked surprised. His jowls shook as he tugged at his collar and twisted his neck. "What do you mean, Alexis?"

"The hatchet job on Dr. Barnes. Is there something going on I need to know about?"

He clamped his jaw shut and focused on the empty air above her head. "I really don't know what you're talking about."

"I'm sorry, Phil, but I can't believe—"

"Do I really have to draw you a picture, Dr. Hartnett? You've seen the budget numbers. Why didn't you consider that before you let Tielman bring another faculty member on board? Barnes is the low man on the totem pole. Think about it."

Alexis stared at him for an uncomfortably long moment, completely unable to frame a response. He pushed past her and opened the door. He half turned his face toward her.

"It's just business."

⤫

"Yes, I'm calling for the dean of our College of Arts and Humanities, Dr. Alexis Hartnett. I'm making some inquiries concerning an application we've received from a Dr. Joe Barnes."

Lucy felt a stab of guilt for the fib, but like most really adroit lies, it actually contained a grain of truth. She kept glancing at Alexis's door, but it had remained firmly closed all morning.

"Hello, ma'am? I have Dr. Barnes's term of employment showing from August 1978 to June 1992. His record indicates he would be eligible for rehire."

Lucy made an impatient face. Of course he was eligible for rehire; she needed something beyond the standard pablum HR departments doled out to keep from getting sued.

*From 1978 to 1992, fourteen years...* "Thank you. Just one more question please. What was Dr. Barnes's rank at the time of his separation?"

"Well, I'm not really supposed to—"

"Yes, I know. I've probably got that on his CV somewhere, but I've misplaced it, and the dean was just wondering..."

"Umm...looks like he had just been promoted to a full professorship, actually."

"Oh, yes, I see it here now. Sorry to bother you."

"That's okay."

"Well, thanks, you've been very helpful."

"No problem."

Lucy hung up. She stared thoughtfully at the phone. Why would a full professor with tenure and fourteen years' seniority suddenly leave his teaching post and go to work outside academia? Joe Barnes's closet definitely housed a skeleton. Lucy just needed to open it and find the light switch.

❧

*Nathaniel Hawthorne inherited a complex legacy. The descendant of a family with a distinguished New England pedigree, he was acutely conscious of his Puritan roots—and not entirely proud of them. As Stephen Vincent Benét was careful to point out in his short story "The Devil and Daniel Webster," a Hawthorne forebear was involved in the notorious Salem witch trials; Benét places "Justice Hathorne" in charge of the diabolical court assembled to hear the famous jurist's arguments. This ancestral figure serves as an unfavorable archetype in several of Hawthorne's works, as is well known. Nathaniel, then, while knowledgeable of (and demonstrably troubled by) his family's past, was at the same time deeply involved in the sweeping intellectual and societal changes taking place in the New England of the early nineteenth century, a movement that would be pivotal in America's eventual shift toward secularism and, according to Stokes,[1] would lay the foundation for much of the modern liberal enterprise.*

*What, then, are we to make of this juxtaposition in the mind of the writer? To a sensitive man, attuned to the most modern trends of emerging Enlightenment thought, what feelings might be provoked by the ghosts of a dark, intolerant—some might even say repressive—past? What sort of expiation or explanation might Nathaniel Hawthorne have sought as he tried to reconcile, in his art and in himself, these two poles of his self-knowledge?*

Joe stared at the page, his eyes flickering back and forth over his opening paragraphs. The provost's comments notwithstanding, this was solid, scholarly inquiry.

Why, then, had the previously apparent support of the committee evaporated as soon as Phil Clement opened his mouth? What had put his proposal on the provost's hit list?

And why did Joe have the vague sense that he somehow deserved it?

He shoved the papers back into his valise and tossed it onto the floor. He glanced at his watch; it was time to leave for the Tielmans'. He wished he were looking forward to the informal gathering. Sophie would be there, and he still wasn't sure of his footing with her. Add the fresh bruising from the fellowship committee, and the past couple of days had placed a severe load on his reserves of self-confidence. Maybe finger foods and a few hands of spades at his department chair's home would be just the ticket.

But somehow he doubted it.

He glanced in the mirror beside his front door and gave half-hearted approval to what he saw there. He picked up the disposable plastic bowl containing his standard offering at bring-your-own-snack gatherings: a block of cream cheese with picante sauce poured over it. He checked the lid to make sure the seal was tight, grabbed his keys, flicked on the outside light, and left.

$\mathscr{IG}$

"Joe! Come on in. Good to see you. Just put your food over there on the counter. Drinks are by the sink in the kitchen, plates and napkins over there. Grab whatever, and find a place to sit." There was a burst of laughter from the den, and Al gave Joe a quick smile as he brushed past him on his way to investigate.

*Poor guy,* Al thought. Joe looked as if he was still stinging from the Thomson committee. Al would've liked to say something encouraging, but anyone who had been at the university for more than a couple of years knew Phil Clement's girth was exceeded only by his ruthlessness. If you were on his to-do list, for whatever reason, it was going to be a bumpy ride.

Sophie had three of the deconstructionists gathered around her, regaling them with some story from a recent road trip to a Modern Language Association regional conference. That explained the laughter; Sophie had a genius for squeezing every last bit of latent humor out of whatever she encountered. Al couldn't count the times he'd seen or heard the exact situation Sophie was telling about and had completely failed to recognize it in her narrative. Her world was just funnier than his somehow.

His wife was standing in the kitchen doorway, waving him over. Barbara asked who else was coming. Al ran down the department roster in his head; Joe had been the only one missing, and he was here now, he told her.

"Why don't you get the tables set up and have everybody divide into teams?" Barbara said. Al turned to obey and felt Barbara's hand on his upper arm.

"And make sure Joe Barnes gets put at the same table as Sophie."

"Oh, for crying out loud, Barbara—"

"Just do it." Her look suggested silence as the wisest response.

Al handed out playing cards and cajoled everybody into teams. He had to pair one of the deconstructionists with Castillo, the woman from the foreign-language faculty they'd needed to make an even number. Al couldn't help but notice the flash of chagrin on Joe's face when he put him with Sophie. *Nice, Barbara.* Though when he thought about it, it might have been Sophie's idea.

Tables were set up in the den, the living room, and the guest bedroom. Al's table cut for deal, and naturally, Bill Schuman won. Bill was the luckiest pessimist Al had ever seen; that's why he'd made sure Bill was his partner. You could almost always count on Bill to win two more tricks than he bid. His only downfall was his refusal to bid nil under any circumstances.

Game was five hundred points; Bill and Al soundly thumped their opponents. But, being a gracious host, Al made suitably self-deprecating noises as they got up from the table to refresh their drinks and snacks and wait for the other games to finish. They were to play the winners from the table in the guest bedroom.

Joe and Sophie.

"Do you guys want to go through the formality of playing us, or do you want to save some time and just concede?" Al asked as the four of them sat.

"Shut up and shuffle," Sophie said, handing the deck to Schuman. "We'll let Bill deal first, but that's the only freebie you're getting. Right, Joe?"

"Oh, ah…sure." Joe gave her a quick smile.

Bill doled out the cards, and Al arranged his hand. "Sophie, your bid," he said.

She opened with a bid of five. Al bid three, and Bill moaned, as Al had known he would. "Come on, Al. I got nothing over here." It was the same thing he'd said in the last hand of the first game when he and Al took all thirteen tricks.

Joe tried to bid two-and-a-half, which earned him an unflattering nickname from his partner. "Okay, three then. But Sophie will have to pull something out of a hat."

"What else is new?" she said. They all laughed, but Al thought there was a little bit of an edge to Sophie's voice.

Bill fussed and fretted and finally bid four. Sophie jotted down the bids and led with an ace of clubs, which went around unmolested.

"Joe, I heard about the committee thing the other day," Bill said. "Sorry. Sounds like the provost sandbagged you."

"Speaking of sandbagging," Sophie said as Bill trumped her next lead, "you bid four with a singleton club?"

Bill gave her an apologetic smile. "Anyway, it's too bad," he said. "Your proposal was good."

"Oh, well. Fortunes of war and all that," Joe said.

"Phil Clement is a no-neck, sneaky, conniving fathead," Sophie said.

"Won the lottery, did you, Sofe?" Al said. Sophie gave him a withering look.

"I feel bad about it too, Joe," he said.

"And I suppose you stood up to Clement in the committee meeting?" Sophie said.

"Now, Sophie," Joe said.

"No, really. What about it, Al? You're Joe's department chair. Did you go to bat for him?"

"Sophie, I don't like Clement any better than you, but you know how he is. Sure, I did my best. But after Clement got through shooting off his mouth, the other chairs practically folded their tents. Even the dean couldn't turn it back the other way—and she tried, believe me." He played a trump, then cursed under his breath, realizing he'd just taken the trick from his own partner. "Sorry, Bill."

"Look, can we talk about something else?" Joe said. "The Thomson fellowship would've been nice, but it's not the end of the world or anything. And who knows? After all, I'm not officially out of the running, right?"

"Whose lead is it anyway?" Al said after the silence had lasted just a fraction too long.

"Yours, Al. Remember? You trumped my ace of hearts," Bill said.

"Oh, yeah. Sorry."

⚘

The game was neck and neck, but Al and Bill finally squeaked past Joe and Sophie, 515–490. From then on it was pretty easy cruising. Especially gratifying to Al was winning the last game of the night from the two deconstructionists he and Bill had beaten in the opening round. They'd worked their way up the loser's bracket back to the finals but were no match for his strategy and Bill's dumb luck.

Al saw Señora Castillo to the door, then went back to the kitchen to help Barbara with the cleanup. Sophie was there, drying plates as Barbara handed them to her.

"Nice party, Al," she said. "You and Barbara put on a good shindig."

"Glad to be of service."

"You and Joe did pretty well," Barbara said.

Al turned away to hide his wince.

"Oh, I don't know," Sophie said. "I don't think his mind was on the game."

"Really? Well, that's too bad."

Al wanted no part of this conversation. "Ah, Barbara, I'm just going to check the den one more time for—"

"Al, you really did back Joe in the Thomson committee, didn't you?" Sophie said.

*Too late.* "Yes, Sophie, I told you. But Clement wasn't having any of it."

"Why do you think the provost wanted to shoot down Joe's chance at a fellowship?" Sophie said.

"If I could figure out why Phil Clement does anything, I'd be dean instead of Alexis."

"Well, it does seem a shame. Everyone speaks so highly of Joe," Barbara said. "Al, you ought to do something."

"Really? And what would that be, I wonder?"

"Well, maybe you could meet with Dr. Hartnett," Sophie said. "You're always going on about needing air cover. Maybe Joe needs a little air cover."

"May I ask why this matter has suddenly become so important to you, Sophie?" Al said.

"Now, Al, you just put that tone of voice back where it came from," Barbara said, pointing a soapy finger at him. "Sophie's concerned about Joe, and that seems very commendable to me. Why don't you try to help instead of looking for ulterior motives?"

"Yes ma'am."

He knew he was beaten, but he didn't have to like it.

# EIGHT

J oe watched as the mechanical arm slid backward. The soapy curtain of the Soak-n-Kleen cycle pattered down on his car, moving toward him across the hood, then over the windshield, then across the top, making a sound like scores of scampering mice.

Joe had a theory that time in a car wash didn't count. You couldn't read, because it was generally too dark. You couldn't talk on a cell phone or listen to music, because you'd be interrupted by the Pow-r-Rinse slamming into the side of the vehicle or the moose-sized blow-dryers. In a car wash, you had nothing else to do but just be; your time was meted out by the machinery, measured off by the cycling of water, soap, and wax. In some obscure way he found this comforting.

He wished he could stop thinking about the Thomson fellowship. What was it really, other than a medallion to demonstrate his worth to the department, a bit of garnish for his vita? Even without the fellowship, he could still write, he could still do the research. He wasn't scheduled to teach in the summer until the second session, starting in July; he'd have time in May and June. He might even be able to get the paper published.

*What would Hawthorne do?* Joe tried to imagine Nathaniel Hawthorne, bewhiskered, dark eyed, and intense, transplanted from the Old Manse at Concord to the bucket seat beside him. Given the on-again, off-again nature of Hawthorne's finances, he would probably tell Joe to concentrate on teaching, since that was paying the bills, and quit worrying about the market volatility of advanced scholarship. What would the creator of Hester Prynne and Reverend Arthur Dimmesdale think if he could see Joe right now?

*It could be worse. I could wind up like a character in one of Hawthorne's novels.*

Joe thought about poor Dimmesdale standing in his pulpit Sunday after Sunday, making his ambiguous, agonized confessions. Or standing on the scaffold under cover of darkness as if such a pantomime of disclosure could deliver his soul from the guilt that stalked his days. It was a real problem, having everyone think you were better than you were.

The dryers whirred up to hurricane force. Water droplets, beaded in tiny domes on the freshly applied wax, fled like a routed army across the hood of the car. Watching idly, Joe realized he was wondering what Alexis Hartnett was doing at this moment.

Maybe he ought to stop dillydallying and ask her out. So what if she was the dean of his college? So what if he might have misread her and would inadvertently offend her by making a personal overture?

So what if, in the next round of budget cuts, she decided to eliminate his position? What was the real downside?

That was the trouble with studying Romantic literature: no matter how right something might feel, you could always think of about a dozen ways it could go wrong.

The green light flashed; the wash cycle was finished. Joe pulled the shift over to D and bumped his way off the car wash's sensor platform. He glanced at the dashboard clock. Eight thirty. Maybe he'd call Dr. Hartnett when he got home, see if she had dinner plans for Friday night.

*Alexis, for Pete's sake. Think of her as Alexis. Give yourself a break for once.*

Alexis slid her hymnal into the rack on the back of the pew in front of her. She settled herself into a listening pose as the minister sorted his notes and looked out over the congregation. He had a half smile playing around his lips, as if he were thinking of a joke that he couldn't admit to knowing. That was something you missed if you were sitting in the back of the church: the expressions on the minister's face. During Dr. Garrett's tenure, that was one of the ways Alexis kept herself awake. Not that his face often changed from his professional scowl.

But Reverend Hughes was different. Despite her better judgment, Alexis had allowed herself to be coerced into sitting on the search committee. The task stopped being drudgery at the precise moment Eli Hughes came for his first interview. The young pastor had been leading a small church somewhere farther north. He was short and stocky, with shoulders and arms that bulged at the seams of his oxford cloth button-down. With a crew cut and bull neck, he looked less like a former seminarian than a former wrestling coach. But his self-deprecating sense of humor, coupled with his impressive ability to articulate a cogent, theologically informed philosophy of ministry, quickly put to rest any questions Alexis harbored about his qualifications to lead a church.

Best of all, he could turn a phrase. Since Eli's coming, Alexis had begun looking forward to the homily. Dr. Garrett had been a wonderful man who had wisely counseled his parishioners through illness, bereavement, wayward children, job losses, and other assorted traumas. Alexis had leaned heavily on him during her own divorce. But the only way to tolerate his sermons was to love and respect him; his oratory didn't stand on its own merits. Not so with Eli Hughes.

"Good morning, everybody," he said and waited. The congregation by now knew what was expected and gave a hearty "Good morning!" back.

"You know, I've always been fascinated by stories of the bizarre, the weird, and the gruesome: the more gruesome, the better, in fact. I guess it has something to do with being the youngest of four boys. Of course, we were a religious home, so that limited my choices. Still, when I was kid, I'll bet I read *Foxe's Book of Martyrs* twenty times—well, honestly, I should probably say I looked at the illustrations twenty times. You know, the line drawings of Saint Sebastian with dozens of arrows in him, and people being lowered onto extra large barbecue grills, and beautiful young women lashed to the backs of wild bulls. You wouldn't believe the degree of religious awe these images inspired in a boy on the cusp of puberty. Don't worry though, parents. I'm not recommending it for the children's curriculum."

Alexis smiled. A ripple of laughter ran through the sanctuary.

"Does anybody know the origin of the word *martyr*? I'll give you a hint: it has nothing to do with anybody's mother-in-law."

A bigger laugh this time. Reverend Hughes gave them the Greek etymology as a lead-in to his central theme: the function of suffering as a witness to the world.

"There's a reason the Christians who died for their faith were called *witnesses,* which is what *martyr* really means. Their suffering was seen, at least in part, as a sort of visual testimony to their confidence in their beliefs. And eventually their willingness to suffer and even die rather than recant their faith led to one of the most sweeping societal changes the world has ever seen.

"The truth is, there's nothing uglier than senseless suffering, but the stranger truth is that suffering endured on behalf of something greater than oneself can be the most beautiful act in the world."

At these words, a memory stirred awake in Alexis, a chance comment Joe had made Friday night as they sat at a small, corner table at Rizzuto's: "I wish I were more convinced of the usefulness of discomfort."

She'd looked at him with a half smile, waiting for the punch line, but it never came.

"I'm not too sure about its usefulness, but I'm pretty convinced of its inevitability," she said finally.

Joe had given a little nod and a sad grin. "But...why?" he said. "After all these millennia of human pain, you'd think we'd have accustomed ourselves to it by now or at least successfully rationalized it. But still we recoil, still every generation has to learn all over again the meaning of misery. It's as though it's the one lesson humanity just can't master. Why is that, do you think?"

Then he looked at her, and something in his eyes made it very difficult for her to keep from stroking his face with her fingertips.

But the moment passed, and he made some self-effacing remark about the brilliance of his dinner repartee, and they laughed and drank their Chianti, and the waiter brought their penne rigate. They ate and talked and groused about students. The conversation was comfortable; it rocked along on its own steam. It was a lovely evening, and at her door Alexis told him so. He smiled and nodded and turned away into the night. No hesitation, no tentative lean in for some obligatory first-date kiss. She watched him walk down her driveway, unsure whether to feel relieved or disappointed.

"And so, friends, the question is, who's willing to be a witness, a martyr, for God?" Reverend Hughes said. "You may not risk death or dismemberment. But what about discomfort? Are you willing to risk that?"

Alexis thought of one of the first times she'd seen Joe Barnes, just after the fall term had begun. She was in the coffee bar around the corner from the front gate of the campus, sitting in the corner nursing a mocha latte. Joe was at the counter, gamely keeping his calm in the face of the trainee cashier's bumbling. Alexis saw him look at the clock; she knew he had an eight o'clock class. When Joe finally had his coffee and his change, he hurried out the door into the swish of the morning traffic. She watched him pace quickly toward campus, his shoulder bag swinging against his side as he tried to hurry without spilling his coffee.

She remembered feeling a little warm glow at his kindness, his patience. Joe refused to shift the burden of his schedule onto the hapless cashier. He was the sort of person who was kind even when he didn't have to be.

*So...whence his existential angst?* she wondered. And then she wondered why she assumed that a kind person would necessarily be an optimistic one.

Alexis looked around the sanctuary at her fellow worshipers. There was poor old Wallace Steigman, seated across the aisle. Wallace was an emeritus even before she came to the university fifteen years ago. He gamely began every sermon in an upright, listening posture but inevitably curled over into an attitude that could pass for reverent humility were it not for his heavy, regular breathing. Since Mrs. Steigman's passing two years ago, there was no one to give him the discreet nudge in the ribs he required to maintain alertness.

It was a comfortable place, this church sanctuary, notwithstanding today's sermon topic. The pews were padded in maroon velvet. The track fixtures amplified the muted light coming through the abstract stained glass just enough to permit the comfortable reading of liturgy or hymnal, and during the prayers someone in the control booth at the back twisted a rheostat until the proper contemplative level was achieved. Winter and summer, the air temperature was maintained at a scrupulously acceptable level. The sound was never too loud or too soft. The church staff and volunteers did everything possible to make the worship experience agreeable.

When had comfort become a prerequisite for approaching God? As Alexis pondered Joe's words and Eli Hughes's message, she found herself nursing a vague disquiet. From what she could recall, when God came among humans, comfort often wasn't high on the agenda. Fire and smoke, yes, and the sound of thunder. And weren't the first words out of the angels' mouths usually "Fear not"? Looking around her, Alexis fancied them saying instead, "Easy, now."

Maybe Joe and Reverend Hughes were onto something important. Maybe discomfort was essential somehow. Now *there* was a message guaranteed to get you invited to parties.

As her minister closed his homily and the congregation shrugged itself upright for the final hymn, Alexis hoped she'd have another chance to hear Joe Barnes's thoughts on this topic. She wouldn't let him shift his ground so easily next time.

# NINE

Lucy sprinkled salt on her hard-boiled egg. She took a bite and chewed thoughtfully. She needed some plausible reason to contact the secretary of Joe Barnes's former department. The background check ploy wouldn't work; the department person would just refer her back to HR.

An annoying voice returned—the one that kept asking her why she was so determined to gather dirt on Joe Barnes. She popped the other half of the egg into her mouth and chewed noisily to drown out the accuser's monotone query. Lucy had a bad feeling about Joe Barnes, and that was it. Nobody saw it but her—certainly not Alexis—and it was up to Lucy to ferret out the truth. The world was full of stinkers, and the most dangerous were the ones who smelled sweetest. She should know.

Poor Polly. If only someone had been watching more closely, Lucy's niece might still be the vibrant, confident girl who'd entered Stanford instead of the diffident, prematurely world-weary twenty-two-year-old who was graduating in the spring. If someone had bothered to notice all the after-hours conferences, the "tutoring sessions" at that awful man's house, Polly might not have been blighted.

The door to the break room opened; it was one of the student workers from payroll. Lucy watched as he went to the refrigerator and retrieved a brown paper sack. He clanked two coins into the honor can and took a soft drink from the top shelf. Lucy turned away, but she still heard the loud, puncturing click of the pull tab and his swallowing sounds. His feet scuffed toward the table. Stephen—that was his name. Or Steve maybe.

"Okay if I sit here?" he said around a mouthful of some kind of sandwich. Lucy gave him a tiny smile and a shrug, and he flopped into the seat across from her.

"Mmfshmx?" He held out a bag of unsalted pretzel sticks toward her.

"Oh, no thank you. I'm just finishing up. I have to get back. Busy, busy."

He nodded as he swallowed. "Yeah, I know. I gotta go from here straight to the library and glue my rear end to a chair." He shoved another bite of sandwich into his mouth.

Lucy creased her napkin into halves, then quarters, then eighths. She dropped it into her brown paper sack, which she folded all the way down until it looked like an oblong envelope. She got up and walked toward the trash can. "Hard semester?" she said as she pressed back the lid and deposited her package.

He rolled his eyes. "Duh. And I totally get no slack from my mom, who knows everything I do apparently. What was I thinking, majoring in accounting when my mom is the department secretary? She's like, practically omniscient." He shook his head as he dug in the bag of pretzel sticks.

*Carlene Willis's son...Steve.* "Your mom's very proud of you, Steve; she's told me so. You're doing fine, I'm sure."

He made a scoffing noise and chomped a mouthful of pretzels. "Maybe. But I still gotta spend the rest of my life in the library."

She pulled her eyes away from the crumbs falling onto the table in front of him and gathered up her lidded plastic bowl and her half-full mug of green tea. "Well, you just work hard, Steve. One day you'll be glad you did."

"Yeah. Maybe I'll make a bunch of money and have them bronze the library chair cushion with my fanny print in it."

Lucy gave him a final smile. She went back to her office, thinking that if she were omniscient, she'd offer him a few pointed suggestions about how to talk to his elders.

He was right about one thing though: departmental secretaries knew everything. From textbook-adoption forms through enrollment figures and even student performance, they had their fingers on the pulse of the university. If Lucy could get a few minutes alone with whoever had been the secretary in Joe Barnes's department at that other school, for example...

Lucy slowed as the thought pooled in her mind. Yes...if it

sounded offhand, an oh-by-the-way kind of thing... Of course, what were the chances the person was still there?

Joe blinked and rubbed his eyes. He *had* to focus on these essays; he'd promised his students they'd have them back tomorrow, and the ungraded stack at his left elbow was still higher than the graded stack at his right. He had the urge to glance at the clock but resisted. If he didn't know how much sleep he was missing, it wouldn't be so hard to get up in the morning. At least, that was what he kept telling himself.

He picked up the next sheaf of stapled, double-spaced sheets. "Walt Whitman—the First Hippie?" he read aloud and groaned. Oh, well. Maybe the argument would be cogent. Or maybe the syntax would be slightly less tortured than the last five attempts he'd plowed through.

He remembered something Alexis had said as they waited for their table last Friday night: "If the administration had to grade freshman essays, the salaries in the English department would triple overnight."

He smiled, thinking of the way she'd leaned toward him as they talked in the noisy waiting area, the way she'd touched his arm while she was speaking to him. And there was that one moment when she looked as if she wanted to touch his face...

Basking in his memories of the evening, he couldn't imagine why he'd been so gun-shy about calling her. Within five minutes of greeting her at the door of her house, he was talking as easily with her as if they'd had years of shared experiences. Which, when he thought about it, maybe they had—only in different places.

*When can I see her again?*

He leaned his forehead into his hand and stared down at the essay. It stared back—a bit truculently, he thought. He sighed and picked up his red pencil. Walt Whitman's reputation—such as it was—was at stake. Joe rubbed his eyes and started to read.

"Phil, this is outrageous!" Alexis flung the memo on the provost's desk. "You can't be serious. I can't do this to my faculty."

Phil Clement leaned back in his chair and bridged his fingertips. "Now, Dr. Hartnett. I can appreciate—"

"You can't actually expect me to walk into a meeting of my department chairs and announce that due to unexpected budget shortfalls, they'll have to lay off faculty before the beginning of the spring term. Faculty, Phil! This is a university. Teaching is what we do. Do you know what kind of havoc this will cause with the class schedules, which have already been published, by the way? Can you imagine how it'll look in the *Journal of Higher Education*?"

"Have you seen the financials for last month, Alexis?"

"Phil, I'm telling you—"

"Have you seen them?"

She clenched her jaw.

"If you had, you'd know that our cash flow is under severe constraints. How would it look in the *Journal* if this university started bouncing checks? Have you considered that?"

She closed her eyes and took a deep breath. "Phil, there has to be some other way."

"I'm just responding to what the VP for finance is saying, Alexis. Personnel is our biggest cost—you know that. We can't stay in the teaching business if we don't pay our bills." He shifted in his chair; the leather upholstery squawked under his weight. "I feel as bad about this as anybody, but it's time to make the hard calls. There's no way around it."

She stared at him, trying hard not to say quite a number of the things she was thinking. He looked back at her, his fat face as placid as the surface of a mountain lake at dawn.

"I want a meeting with all the deans and the president, Phil. I won't ask my faculty to make this kind of sacrifice."

Phil leaned forward and aimed a pudgy finger at her. "Then I will, Dr. Hartnett. I'll ask them. And it'll happen, with or without your meeting of the deans. Do you honestly think the president doesn't know what we're facing? Do you think you're the only dean who has to have some unpleasant conversations? Come on, Alexis. You're an administrator. Administrate."

He never raised his voice; his brow never furrowed. It was the way Alexis imagined a serial killer would look to the victim just before plunging in the blade. He saw the financials as an accounting problem. She saw faces.

"I need revised budgets for each department on my desk before Christmas break," Clement said. "There can be no variance from the allocation shown in the memo. Was there anything else, Dr. Hartnett?" He looked down and began scribbling on a notepad.

She studied the top of the provost's head and then the brass-and-marble paperweight by his right elbow. Then she turned and walked out, slamming the door behind her.

Al Tielman's eyes widened as he read. He lowered the memo and stared at Alexis with a stricken expression. "This has to be done by next semester?"

Alexis nodded.

"But the class schedules—"

"Have already been published. Yes. I pointed that out to the provost."

He puffed out his cheeks. "I knew things were a little tight, but…"

In the silence that followed, Alexis's door opened, and Lucy stepped softly to her desk. She handed Alexis a one-page spreadsheet and went back out, closing the door behind her. Alexis looked at the spreadsheet a moment, then slid it across her desk to Al.

"Here's a listing of your department, ranked by seniority. Salaries are shown in the last column to the right."

Al took the paper as if it were laced with anthrax powder. He swallowed and nodded.

"Make your cuts—your recommendations—and bring it back to me early next week. We'll have to start telling people pretty soon after that. They need time to...make plans."

He looked at her. "I'm sorry, Alexis."

"Me too."

"No, I mean...I'm really sorry."

"I know, Al. I am too."

"Okay." He got up and walked out, looking everywhere but at the spreadsheet in his hand.

Alexis had her head in her hands when she heard the door open again. Lucy was standing there.

"Dr. Hartnett, I thought I should tell you...I'm taking a personal day on Friday."

"Fine, Lucy. Just get a student worker to cover the phone."

"Already did. I'm...going to just have a little time by myself, if that's okay."

"It's fine, Lucy. That's why they call them personal days."

"Yes, well...just wanted you to know."

Alexis nodded and put her head back in her hands. The door closed.

Joe handed the essay back to the tall kid. He reached to take it, and his arm seemed to stretch halfway across the room. The paper had a red B circled at the top.

"Good work, Jamal. I liked the way you used quotes from your subject's contemporaries to back up your main ideas. Your writing has really come along this semester. Thanks for the great effort."

Jamal gave Joe a sideways, slightly embarrassed smile and bent his head to look at his paper. His hands were nearly as big as the eight-and-a-half-by-eleven sheets. Joe moved on to the next student.

These papers were, as a group, better than those turned in early in the term. Not all, unfortunately, had worked as hard as Jamal to improve their writing or analytical skills. But most had shown at least some progress. Joe felt good about this class.

In fact, Joe realized, he felt good about everything. He'd awakened this morning with Alexis's face on his mind. For the first time in a while, he was looking forward more often than looking back. It was a nice feeling.

Joe glanced at his watch. "Okay, folks, that's it for today. Remember to check the finals schedule before next week. We'll do some review the next couple of classes. Have a good afternoon, everybody."

He watched them load their backpacks and gather their books, wishing that Alexis were standing in his doorway as she had been that day a few weeks ago. This time he wouldn't be so shy about asking her to share lunch.

But when he turned toward the door, Al Tielman was there, and he was looking at Joe with an expression that was anything but inviting.

# TEN

"Hey, Al. What's up?"

Tielman ducked his head like someone digging deep for something to say, but he came up empty.

"Joe, I...we have to talk."

Joe forced a smile. "Whoa. If we were dating, I'd take that as a bad opening."

"Yeah, well... You got some time now?"

"Sure, sure. I have office hours, then lunch. You want to grab something to eat?"

Tielman gave him a guilty look. "Uh, no. Thanks."

"Okay then." They reached Joe's office, and he gestured Al through the doorway with a hospitality he was feeling less and less as the moments passed. He set his valise in the corner and took a seat in front of the desk. He motioned at the other chair, but Al shook his head. He was rubbing his hands on the sides of his pants as if something was on his palms that he couldn't get rid of.

"Joe, I've just come from a meeting with the dean—"

*She hates me.*

"I can't believe this, but…"

*I offended her over dinner, and she's telling everybody what a jerk I am.*

"Apparently, some things have been going on that none of us knew about."

*She's dismissing me immediately and putting out a contract to have me dropped in a river somewhere.*

"The provost's office sent out a memo saying that because of budget problems, we have to cut payroll by twelve percent…before the beginning of the spring semester."

*Okay, that's actually worse than I thought.* "In the middle of the academic year?"

Al nodded. He looked like he'd just swallowed something sharp.

The silence that followed was uncomfortable. But, Joe realized, not as uncomfortable as whatever words would follow it. Al was still standing. Should Joe stand so he could take the mortal blow as an equal? Or should he continue to sit, like a condemned man in the electric chair?

"Well, I am the newest hire, Al—last one to the dance."

Al nodded, then sank weakly into the chair. Joe thought he saw a trace of something like gratitude. He guessed it wasn't often the victim administered his own *coup de grâce*.

"I feel just rotten about this, Joe. You're a fantastic teacher, an asset to the department."

"And a pretty fair boccie player."

Al nodded and aimed a weak smile at the floor.

"Let me guess: my salary makes up, oh, say, twelve percent of the department's payroll?"

"Eleven point eight."

"Yeah. Pure coincidence, I'm sure. So...how will you cover my classes for next semester? Schuman'll take Modern American, I guess?"

"Probably. I haven't gotten that far yet."

"I don't suppose you'll be needing any adjunct teachers?"

"The way Alexis—the dean made it sound, we can't even afford staplers."

"I'm really sorry, Al. This must be terribly hard."

"Are you kidding me? I'm laying you off, and you're feeling sorry for me?"

Joe shrugged. "Better than feeling sorry for myself, which I'll likely do soon enough."

"Look, Joe, you know I'll give you the highest recommendation in the world—"

"Which will be very helpful, probably, next July or so." He gave Tielman a sad smile. "But who's going to be hiring English profs at Christmastime?"

Al rubbed his face and stood. "Well, I should probably go so you can start cursing and throwing things." He moved toward the door, then half turned back to Joe. "If there's anything—"

"Yeah, Al. Thanks. I know."

Tielman left. Joe stared at the chair where he had been.

*So this is what downsizing feels like.*

Joe wondered when the loneliness would come crashing in, the sense of being out on his own with no resources. That had been the worst part of the divorce: realizing no one had his back. Of course, if he was honest, he had to admit that Carol hadn't had his back for some years, just as he hadn't had hers. Still, when it became official, the feeling of isolation got worse. Joe remembered being surprised by that. He'd thought the judge's decree would be more like the period at the end of a sentence. It wasn't.

He thought about Alexis then and wished he could go talk to her. But what would be the point? This had come across her desk; there was nothing she could do. Even if she wanted to.

*Does she want to?*

Joe stared at the books on the shelf above his desk and, against his better judgment, let his mind run over some of the more frightening possibilities for the next few weeks. At least he hadn't signed the lease on that little two-bedroom house near the campus. He had a little money saved up, but the rent on his apartment would quickly become a challenge after the paychecks stopped.

And when would that be exactly? Al hadn't given him much detail. A memo would probably come around, something from Human Resources that attached an innocuous term to the fact of his firing.

"Fired. I've been fired. Discharged. Sacked. I'm about to become a former assistant professor of English."

Nope. Naming the demon didn't seem to help. Joe still felt the vague beginnings of panic trying to gain a purchase in his throat. He decided to take a walk. He reached for his topcoat and wool cap. Less than fifteen minutes ago he'd been feeling great. What was the reason for the difference, really? he wondered. It wasn't likely he'd starve. He didn't have a pack of creditors to keep at bay. There was probably enough freelance editing work, combined with his savings, to keep him afloat until the next academic hiring season. What was the actual downside?

He had a sudden image of himself whistling his way through a graveyard at midnight.

He walked down the carpeted hallway, hands thrust into his coat pockets. He heard the murmur of voices through the walls: colleagues lecturing, students asking questions. He heard the click of computer keys coming from the department secretary's door, always open. He heard the low hum of the fluorescent bulbs in the fixtures above his head. He stopped walking and listened to the whir of the academic machine, continuing unabated all around him, and he realized that at this moment, he would give almost anything to feel himself a part of it still rather than an outsider. So what if the knowledge he shoved at his students seemed to most of them like a hurdle to be crossed? Teaching was what he could do; it was something worthwhile. And it paid the bills. Why did it have to be taken away now just as he was allowing himself to relish it again?

*It had to happen. You knew it would as soon as you started to admit you were enjoying life again.*

*Who says? Who made the rule about smacking down happiness?*

*Nobody made the rule. It's always been there.*

*I don't believe that.*

*Don't you?*

Joe went to the elevator, then decided to use the stairs. It would give his adrenaline something to do besides ramp up emotions.

It was probably stupid anyway, this whole notion of walking around with a cosmic bull's-eye on his chest. Who said the universe cared one way or another about his comfort or the lack thereof? What made him special enough to be the chosen target of…

Of what exactly? Or whom? Or Whom? Surely God had better things to do than aim the slings and arrows of outrageous fortune at Joe Barnes. In the eternal scheme of things, Joe figured he had to be reasonably small potatoes.

He pushed against the dull silver bar of the glass door and stepped into the duller gray of the December noontime. He ambled across the brittle brown grass of the quadrangle, heading in some general way for the student union building and the cafeteria, maybe a bowl of the soup of the day.

*Can I afford the soup of the day?*

Alexis's building was to his left. He didn't want to look at it, didn't want to think about her. Not now.

*One dinner doesn't change this. One pleasant conversation doesn't mean she can do anything to bail you out. She's responsible for a whole college. At least show enough respect for yourself and for her to remember that.*

❧

Alexis jabbed at the remote. Violetta's voice vanished in the middle of her aria, and the sinuous glide of John Coltrane's tenor sax filled the room. What was she thinking, listening to Verdi in her present mood?

She resettled her glasses on her nose and looked again at the papers she'd received back from her department chairs. What was she looking for? Some way to avoid the inevitable? Something that Al Tielman and the others might have missed? Some magical detour past her most distasteful act since becoming dean?

She'd added the numbers a dozen times already. She'd divided, subtracted, and averaged. No matter how many times she manipulated the figures, it always came back to the identical sum: she would have to authorize the layoffs of people she didn't think her college could do without. And one of them was Joe Barnes.

Alexis tossed the papers aside and flung herself up from the couch. She wandered toward the kitchen, the shush of Philly Joe Jones's brushes syncopated by the click of her pumps across the hardwood floor. She reached into her fridge and pulled out a bottle of Pinot Grigio. The cork twisted and broke in her fingers. Suppressing the impolite word that formed immediately in her mind, she tried to work a corkscrew into the damaged cork, only to have the whole thing fall down into the bottle and float like a jaunty, miniature coracle atop the straw-colored wine.

*Oh, well. Not that much left in the bottle. Might as well finish it.* She poured slowly, keeping the rogue cork out of the bottle's neck, then carried the bottle and her glass back into the den. Lee Morgan was just beginning his trumpet solo, riffing up and down scales and arpeggios atop the steady thumping of Philly Joe and the smooth, low ticking of Paul Chambers's bass.

There was a cynical wistfulness to blues music from the late fifties and early sixties. None of the exhibitionist yowling of the primitive singers from the early years, and still too early for the disjointed chaos of free improvisation. Cool jazz was her favorite: the predictable flow of the rhythm section and the linear, throwaway improvisations of the soloists. Enough structure to provide comfort, and enough freedom to allow expression.

Alexis wished she could reach as high as wistfulness. She wished she could climb atop one of Coltrane's looping, undulating rides and live there until the hard conversations had come and gone, until the unpleasantness was over. She wished the next few days could somehow just flash by undetected, leaving her on the other side, as cool and collected as the clusters of notes plunked out by Kenny Drew's right hand.

*I will have to speak to Joe Barnes about this. I will have to look him in the eye and listen to whatever he decides to say to me. I will have to see him, and I will have to despise myself for a very long time afterward.*

In all the hundreds of conversations she'd had with herself about why she shouldn't allow herself to be in love with Joe Barnes, this situation was one she hadn't permitted herself to envision. Why not?

*Because I didn't want to. Because I had some stupid, girlish hope that the magic between us would take care of everything else, that daily life wouldn't be strong enough to come between us. How old am I anyway? How old do you have to be to finally know that hope isn't always enough, that life happens, no matter how much you care?*

Alexis thought about the night she and Brooks told the children about the impending divorce. They'd managed to drag the marriage along until all the kids were out of high school. But then it came time to have "the talk," and in good, sportsmanlike fashion, they'd decided to do it together, all at once.

Jamie had started crying first. That surprised Alexis. Her devil-may-care, free-spirited nineteen-year-old had never given her reason to believe life could lay a glove on him. He took everything in stride, Jamie did. Being dumped unceremoniously in junior high by his girlfriend of two years, flunking the written portion of his driving test on his first attempt, failing to be cast in the senior play—it all rolled off him like water off a duck's back. But when Brooks said the words, "Your mother and I need to tell you that, unfortunately, we've decided…" Jamie's head dropped, and his shoulders began shaking.

Alexis remembered wishing for a time slide, a swooping, tummy-flipping descent to the bottom so they could quickly begin the climb back to normal life—whatever that was going to be. But with each muffled sob from her son's throat, time seemed to apply its brakes. It crystallized around her like a cocoon, or a sarcophagus. The moment stretched on and on without relief as Jamie wept out his despair.

He was too big to pull into her lap even if he would permit such a thing. She looked at Jenny and Cara, and the girls' eyes were on their father's face, waiting in somber silence, too respectful or shocked to do anything but listen to Brooks's prepared remarks.

Brooks was good at this sort of thing. He could script a difficult conversation, then stick to the script. Despite Alexis's best attempts at saying only what she had thought out, she was constantly darting to this side and that, improvising madly with every change in body language, every real or perceived reaction from her listener. She was content to let Brooks handle this one. There was little enough to say anyway. What sort of explanation or amplification could she offer her children for her part in their parents' failure to keep their most basic promise? What could she say that would make any difference?

It was the same way now. The inevitability of the conversation she was going to have with Joe Barnes and with everyone else whose careers would be sidelined felt like a sour taste in her mouth that nothing could rinse away. It was like the onset of nausea; you knew what was coming, and you wished you could avoid it, but you also knew that there was no way out except through the heaving and retching that waited in your future like a buzzard waits for a dying animal.

*What can I say, Joe? What can I tell you that will make the slightest bit of difference?*

# ELEVEN

The pictures in the worn, creased copy of *People* reminded Lucy of a high-school yearbook. Not the class pictures, ranked on their pages like windows in a prison wall. No, the candid shots had always been her favorites: a couple captured in midgyration at the homecoming dance, snapshots of overly solemn National Honor Society officers at the podium, crowd shots of the bleachers at a football game with everyone trying not to notice the photographer. That was how the young and beautiful looked in *People:* they studiously ignored the camera's eye even as it further guaranteed the marketability of their principal assets.

By this point in the lunch hour, the faculty-staff lounge was sparsely populated. Lucy had been waiting since half past noon. She glanced at her watch and shifted the limp magazine pages back and forth. Her back ached from the drive, and the avocado green vinyl chair she occupied looked to be the most comfortable in the room, unfortunately.

The door swung open, and an older woman peered inside. "Are you…Lucy?"

As soon as she heard the woman's voice, Lucy knew her trip hadn't been in vain. From the look of her, from the proprietary way she glanced around the lounge, Lucy sensed she'd been at this university a long time. Departmental secretaries acquired a certain presence with longevity. Tenured professors deferred to them; assistant professors feared them.

"Yes, I'm Lucy. You must be Mrs. Hanks. Thank you so much for meeting with me on such short notice."

Mrs. Hanks made a dismissive gesture. "Well, do you want to talk here or in my office?"

"Your office would be fine." *And maybe there are some decent chairs there.*

"Now, what was it I was supposed to show you?"

"Oh, you don't need to show me anything, Mrs. Hanks. My dean is compiling figures on faculty turnover for a study, and one of our professors suggested you'd be a good source of anecdotal material."

Mrs. Hanks peered over her bifocals at Lucy. "Who do you know that knows me?"

"Well, Dr. Joe Barnes used to teach here, and he said that you—"

"Dr. Barnes? Really? I haven't heard from him in a while."

"He's…a great admirer of yours." It was probably true, after all. Butter wouldn't melt in Joe Barnes's mouth; Lucy was sure he'd find something good to say about anybody if that was what he thought a person wanted to hear.

Mrs. Hanks gestured Lucy through the doorway of her office, a desk crammed into the alcove in front of a closed door that, Lucy presumed, opened onto the department head's inner sanctum. There was just enough room inside the doorway for the chair in front of Mrs. Hanks's desk. It was one of those upholstered affairs built on a steel S-frame; sitting in it, Lucy had the feeling she might tip over backward.

"How long have you been here, Mrs. Hanks?"

"Oh, honey, I quit counting years ago."

Lucy gave her a tight smile. "Time does fly, doesn't it?"

Mrs. Hanks rolled her eyes.

"Now, can I ask you a few questions?" Lucy laid her legal pad on the desk and fished in her purse for a pen.

"Shoot."

"All right, let's see… In your time with this department, about how often would you say faculty members who left the university didn't have tenure?"

"Hmm. Never really considered that, I don't guess. Most of 'em leave either because they didn't get tenure or because they got a better offer somewhere else before they had a chance for tenure here. Umm… Oh, I'd say that happens probably at least half the time. No, more than that… Say, eighty percent of the time."

"I see." Lucy scribbled on her pad. "So most of the faculty who leave this university, at least, don't have tenure."

"Oh, sure. The majority, I'd say."

"All right then. So my logical next question is, how many leave after receiving tenure?"

"That's less frequent, certainly."

"That's what I'd expect," Lucy said. "In our university we rarely see tenured faculty leave."

Mrs. Hanks nodded. "Yeah, it takes something out of the ordinary. Now and then somebody will get a great offer from another school. Or…something else."

"I'm curious, Mrs. Hanks. What would 'something else' be?"

Mrs. Hanks gave her a strange look.

"Just curious," Lucy said, giving what she hoped looked like a carefree shrug.

"Oh…could be they get crossways with the administration or a colleague. They could just be burned out on teaching—though by the time they've been granted tenure, they've usually worked their way through that tendency. And every now and then, you get an ethics situation."

"Ethics?"

"Sure, you know, teacher-student romance, that kind of thing."

"Hmm. Is that a problem here?"

"No more here than anywhere else." Mrs. Hanks gave her a no-

nonsense look. "And not something we discuss with people taking polls."

"Oh, no, of course not. I mean, we all have these little secret situations, don't we?"

Mrs. Hanks stared at her, and Lucy quickly scratched more lines on her paper. She let a few moments crawl by, doing stage business with her notepad. When she judged the air had cooled sufficiently, she said, "Mrs. Hanks, how often would you say you have teachers come here from somewhere besides another university? Other than first-time instructors, I mean."

Mrs. Hanks studied the air above Lucy's head. "Almost never, I'd say. We typically see the usual career track: graduate degree, doctorate, some assistantships during the graduate work, and teaching experience at one or more other colleges or universities. We don't see too many professors coming from outside the academic world."

"That's interesting. You know, Dr. Barnes came to us from a publishing house."

Mrs. Hanks stared at Lucy long enough to make her uncomfortable. "What's this got to do with faculty turnover?"

"Nothing really. Just that…we try to look at all the factors related to our professors' credentials and employment history," Lucy said, doing her best to meet Mrs. Hanks's eyes evenly. "If there's anything out of the ordinary, we think it's our job to wonder why."

"And you think there's something wrong with Joe Barnes."

Lucy gave a noncommittal shrug and underlined a few of the random words on her notepad.

Mrs. Hanks pointed a finger at Lucy. "Dr. Barnes was completely exonerated of all charges of misconduct," she said. "He left here with a clean record. Clean. Understand?"

Lucy nodded, wide eyed and innocent. "Oh, of course. I hope I didn't imply—"

"He's a decent human being and a fine teacher. You're lucky to have him."

"Well…thank you."

"Are you finished?"

Lucy's neck was starting to burn, but she did her best imitation of someone studying her notes and considering what else she might need to ask. "Yes, I guess that about covers it," she said finally, pushing her chair back and standing up.

"That's what I thought." Mrs. Hanks stayed in her seat and gave her a look that reminded Lucy of someone staring at a cockroach.

She gave Mrs. Hanks a bright smile and held out her hand. "Well, thank you very much for your time, Mrs. Hanks."

Mrs. Hanks just kept looking at her. Lucy retracted her hand and ducked quickly through the door.

"I'm sure you can find the way out," Mrs. Hanks called after her.

Lucy was sure she could. Now all she had to do was figure out how to make the best use of what she had. With just the right touch, she thought, it would be enough.

*꒜*

The Reverend Mr. Dimmesdale bent his head, in silent prayer, as it seemed, and then came forward.

"Hester Prynne," said he, leaning over the balcony, and looking down steadfastly into her eyes, "thou hearest what this good man says, and seest the accountability under which I labor.... Be not silent from any mistaken pity and tenderness...for, believe me, Hester, though he were to step down from a high place, and stand there beside thee. on thy pedestal of shame, yet better were it so, than to hide a guilty heart through life...."

Hester shook her head.

"Woman, transgress not beyond the limits of Heaven's mercy!" cried the Reverend Mr. Wilson, more harshly than before. "...Speak out the name! That, and thy repentance, may avail to take the scarlet letter off thy breast."

"Never!" replied Hester Prynne....

"She will not speak!" murmured Mr. Dimmesdale, who, leaning over the balcony, with his hand upon his heart, had awaited the result of his appeal. He now drew back, with a long respiration. "Wondrous strength and generosity of a woman's heart! She will not speak!"

Joe shook his head. No matter how many times he read *The Scarlet Letter,* Dimmesdale always made him want to gargle with turpentine.

He spent the first part of the story worrying about getting caught and the last part whining about guilt.

Even Hawthorne, from his omniscient vantage point, seemed to allow the illicit paramours the purity of their love once they got out into the forest and away from the tut-tutting of the community. He seemed to share the couple's covert belief that their only shame was violating the Puritan sexual ethic.

Joe tossed the book onto his nightstand and snapped off his bedside lamp. He yawned and rubbed his eyes, then stared up at the ceiling, waiting for his pupils to dilate.

Why was repentance so hard? Or was it just out of fashion?

The glow from the streetlight outside his window filtered through the half-open miniblinds, striping the opposite wall in a pattern that made him think of the prison bars in a James Cagney movie. It was sort of like moonlight but too strong and a little too yellow.

When Kim came to his house, the moon had been full.

He should've pretended not to notice the way she looked at him in class. He could be lecturing on Henry James, and still she would drink him in, her eyes glittering like wet, chestnut-colored pebbles set in a face far too knowing for a woman of twenty-three.

Joe wanted to believe it would've mattered if things had been better between him and Carol, but sometimes he wondered. How could a man see that hunger of body, mind, and spirit staring back at him and remain unaffected? That was probably what tormented him the most. What was the essential difference between himself and Dimmesdale, agonizing over some mirage of co-victimhood? He hadn't actually *meant* for anything to happen, so somehow that made it okay, right?

Wrong. In the dark and the stillness, with no witness but the red LED face of his alarm clock, it was harder to see himself as the righteous-but-susceptible figure who had graciously weathered the quiet storm in his former department or as the regretful, mostly innocent partner in a dissolving marriage. He could see nothing but the relative shambles his life had become; he could do nothing but sift through the wreckage for shards of fault to scratch the boils on his conscience.

One of the things he had enjoyed when he first moved to New York was the constant rush and buzz, the raw energy of so many humans and machines in such a tight space. Walking past Penn Station or down West Sixty-second Street, you could almost forget those voices that only found you in the silent spaces of your mind. Going to a busy office where everybody was on an impossible deadline all the time, you could almost drown the inner accuser in the constant riptide of adrenaline.

Almost.

Joe wanted to call Alexis but realized his cell phone was in the other room. Turning on the light and going to look for it seemed too volitional. Too exposed.

He tried to imagine what she might say. Would she offer words of comfort? Would he hear the welcome in her voice, feel the space between the two of them that was as right and comfortable as his own skin?

He didn't know, didn't even know what he'd want her to say. He didn't like to think of approaching her as a supplicant.

What if she knew everything about him, even the secrets he tried to keep from himself?

He tried to shut his eyes and his mind. He took deep breaths: seven counts in, seven out. Eight counts in, eight out. He recited Antony's funeral speech from *Julius Caesar*. He said the Lord's Prayer.

He rolled over and looked at his clock. Two twenty a.m.

It was going to be a long night.

# TWELVE

Lucy was at her desk bright and early, and that was no small task. The drizzle that had begun falling as she drove back into town the evening before had frozen during the night; the trees on campus looked as if they'd been dipped in spun sugar. The streets were treacherous, and she had to crawl along to keep control of her car. Still, there was no possibility that she wouldn't be here.

In fact, the ice storm had turned to her advantage, Lucy decided. Not everyone was as determined as she; the building was quiet, and the phone, which usually played havoc with her concentration, was largely silent. The sigh of the heating vent and the muted gargle of the two-cup coffee maker on her credenza made a soothing, focusing backdrop for her contemplation of the memo taking shape on her computer screen.

FROM: Lucille M. Conn, Office of the Dean of Arts
        and Humanities

TO:

Lucy hadn't really decided where this should go. The provost's office was a good bet from what she'd heard through the grapevine. But why would a dean's administrative assistant send a sensitive communication directly to the provost? Of course, there was no possibility of taking the matter to Dr. Hartnett. Lucy had stewed on this awhile and decided to leave that part blank. The right answer would come to her in time.

SUBJECT: Potential Ethical Impropriety by a Faculty Member

MESSAGE: In the course of research to complete the personnel dossier on a member of the Arts and Humanities faculty, evidence was found of a prior investigation into a questionable relationship possibly existing between the subject, who subsequently became employed at this university, and a student at the university where the subject was previously employed. These events took place prior to the subject's hiring here, but in accordance with this university's strict policy of protecting its students, faculty, and staff from unwanted and unethical sexual advances, I thought it incumbent upon me to raise this issue so that a full investigation might occur and all facts of the matter could become known to those responsible for protecting the integrity and reputation of this university.

The cursor blinked to the right of the period following "university." Lucy was calculating the chances of anything she'd written so far being demonstrably false. There was nothing in Joe Barnes's vita or personnel records to indicate the events alluded to by Mrs. Hanks, but that didn't surprise Lucy. That wasn't how such things worked, in Lucy's experience. She'd be willing to bet that her niece's professor was still gainfully employed, still lecturing and leering, going right ahead with his life as though nothing had happened—as though he hadn't damaged Polly in ways no one could imagine. No, there wouldn't be anything on Joe Barnes's résumé; all traces would have been wiped clean. Nice and tidy.

Well, not this time. Lucy would see to it. Joe Barnes's sins would be yanked into the open for everyone—especially Alexis Hartnett—to see. So what if he was going to be laid off at the end of this semester. Sooner or later he'd find himself another job to crawl into, another place to snare vulnerable women with his good looks and his charming smile. Lucy meant to deprive Joe Barnes of every bit of camouflage he'd ever scrounged. Everyone would see him for what he really was.

*What about "innocent until proven guilty"?*

*By the time guilt is proven, the damage is already done! Now, will you please either help me or leave me alone?*

The coffee maker gave a long, rattling gasp. Lucy pulled the carafe from the hot plate and poured her mug full of the dark, steaming tea. She slid out the brewing compartment, plucked up the tea bag by its string, and dropped it into the trash can. The smell of Darjeeling always made Lucy think of rain forests. She added honey, squeezed a wedge of lemon, and stirred, then cupped the warm mug in her hands and continued to study her memo, inhaling the vapor as it rose from her tea.

$\mathscr{L}$

"I am *not* a pessimist," Bill Schuman said. "It's just that reality actually does suck, and I'm the only one who admits it."

"Yeah, right, Bill. You're the only person I know who chuckles while reading Camus." Sophie took a tangerine out of her pocket and started peeling.

"You gotta read him in French," Schuman said. "The English translations are all so dark."

"Well, all I know is that I'd rather have eaten one of my own ears than tell Joe Barnes his job ends with the semester," Tielman said. "Poor guy. Didn't get the Thomson fellowship, and now he's out on his keister."

Schuman shook his head and tsked.

"You think eating your ear might have helped the budget?" Sophie said.

"Bet they could've sold quite a few tickets for that," Schuman said.

"Could've sold more if you'd eaten the provost's," Sophie said.

The door of the faculty commons swung open, and Joe Barnes came in. The three fell silent. He glanced at them. "I can't tell you how your morbid fascination flatters me," he said.

"Umm...you want some tangerine?" Sophie held the uneaten half toward him.

He gave her a sad smile. "No, trying to cut down, thanks." He turned toward the cabinet and reached for a mug. "Though I might take a rain check come about January."

Tielman looked like someone who'd just stepped in manure and was hoping no one would notice. "Hi, Joe. How's...it going." He grimaced and mimed a pistol shot to his head.

"Nice one, Al," Sophie said. "I have a little salt over here if you want some to sprinkle in Joe's wound."

"It's okay, Sophie," Joe said, stirring his coffee. "I really wouldn't know how to act if you guys started being nice to me just because I'm fired and all."

"Oh, come on! A little decorum, at least!"

"Relax, Al," Sophie said. "Try to pretend this isn't about you."

"What are you going to do, Joe?" Schuman said.

Joe took a long sip of coffee. "Not sure," he said. "Guess I'll get in touch with some of my former colleagues at Harper, see if they can toss me some freelance work. Maybe I'll check around with some of the other schools nearby. Possibly they could use me as an adjunct. And I guess there's always substitute teaching."

The three groaned in unison.

"Beats hunger," Joe said.

"Not by much," Schuman said.

"No, that's great, Joe," Sophie said. "You're on the canvas, and the ref is counting. And still, you're pulling it together to stand up one more time, to take your best shot. I admire you, kid. You got guts."

"Yes, well…thanks for that rousing encouragement, there, Gipper," Joe said. "And now, if you'll excuse me, I have a little more ignorance to stamp out." He started toward the door.

"Seriously, Joe, if there's anything…anything at all," Tielman said.

"I know, Al. Thanks. I really do appreciate it. And I know you'd rather have done almost anything than tell me what you did."

Schuman covered his ears with his palms. Sophie barked with laughter. Joe looked at them quizzically. Tielman waved him off. "Never mind, Joe. These two have no respect whatever."

Joe smiled and shook his head, then went out.

"You gotta admit," Schuman said, pointing at the door with his chin, "that's one classy guy."

"Yeah," Tielman said, nodding.

Sophie stared at the place where Joe had been. After a while, Schuman and Al both looked at her.

"What?" she said.

"Something's going on in your head, Sofe," Al said. "I can smell the gears burning."

"None of your business," she said, wrinkling her nose at him. "Besides, if you knew everything I was thinking, you might decide to fire me. And then I'd be forced to kill you, and where would that leave us?"

"With two vacancies in the department," Schuman said.

"You're right. That could actually solve Joe's problem…" Sophie leaned back thoughtfully and popped a tangerine wedge into her mouth. "Now if I could just figure out how to solve mine…"

"I'd hire a bodyguard, Al," Schuman said.

"Maybe Joe'd do it," Tielman said.

"Beats substitute teaching," Sophie said.

The three of them nodded.

☙

The knock on his doorframe pulled Joe's eyes away from the screen of his laptop. He looked at the young, thin man in the ill-fitting tweed sports coat for a moment, then smiled and gestured at the chair in front of his desk. He fingered the Save command on his keyboard; he didn't want to lose the final exam he'd been working on all morning. He closed the laptop and reached across the desk to shake the young man's hand.

"Hi, I'm Joe Barnes. How can I help you?"

"Yes, Dr. Barnes. I'm Lance, from over in HR."

"Oh, sure." Joe gave him a sad smile. "I guess you're here to tell me how many more paychecks I can expect before…" He drew a finger across his throat.

Lance shifted in his chair and looked away, through the open doorway. "No, Dr. Barnes, I don't work in the payroll area. I'm here on…another errand."

"Okay." Joe leaned back in his chair and clasped his hands in front of him. "Whatever you need. Shoot."

Lance gave him an odd look, then studied the contents of a folder in his lap. "Dr. Barnes, I'm here to inform you that an ethics investigation has been instituted to inquire into certain matters of your previous employment."

Joe gave him a confused look. "A what?"

"Specifically, Dr. Barnes, we're looking into some circumstances that occurred at your former teaching position, prior to your work at, ah…Harper and Row, I believe it was? It seems we need to clear up some uncertainties before we can complete your separation file here."

Lance slid the file across the desk. Joe peered at the memo lying across the open folder. "A questionable relationship…unethical sexual advances…" He looked at Lance. The heading at the top was blacked out with permanent marker. "Where'd this come from?"

"We have to investigate allegations from any reliable source; university policy is very clear on that. We've made some inquiries." Lance pulled a pad from the inside pocket of his coat and referred to it. "Does the name Kim DiCarlo sound familiar?"

Joe felt his face going stiff; he heard his pulse hammering in his ears. To hear that name spoken aloud after all this time…

"But that was all resolved years ago. Kim—Ms. DiCarlo—told the committee nothing happened, and that's the absolute truth. My file reflects that, doesn't it?"

Lance looked at him as if he'd just recited the opening stanzas of *Beowulf* in Old English. "Not quite, Dr. Barnes. There are some ambiguities. And before we can complete your separation here, we need to tie up all these, ah, loose ends."

"So…even though I'm fired at the end of this semester—"

"Separated."

"Fine. Separated at the end of this semester, you still have to dig into a bunch of stuff that happened more than ten years ago—"

"Twelve years and eight months," Lance said, referring to his notepad.

"To do what? Keep me from getting my final paycheck? What's the point of all this?"

"It's very important that your records be complete and accurate at your separation," Lance said, pulling the file back across the desk and folding it together. "We don't want to provide an incomplete or misleading work history to a future potential employer."

Joe looked at him, open mouthed.

Lance tapped the closed folder on the desk and stood up. "You'll be contacted by a representative of the Professional Ethics Committee. This is your formal notice of the investigation. Good day." He quickly left the room.

Joe didn't know if he wanted to laugh, cry, or drink a quart of formaldehyde. After a while he picked up his phone. He stared at the touch pad for maybe twelve seconds, then dialed Alexis's extension.

"Dean's office."

"Dr. Hartnett, please."

"I'm sorry; she just stepped out."

"When will she return?"

"I'm sorry; she didn't say."

"Can you put me in her voice mail?"

"I'll be glad to take a message."

A pause.

"Hello? Did you want to leave a message?"

"No, umm...Lucy, right?"

"Yes, this is Lucy."

"Hi, Lucy. This is Joe Barnes."

"Yes, Dr. Barnes, I recognized your voice."

"Oh, well, thanks, I...guess..."

"Did you want me to take a message, Dr. Barnes? Dr. Barnes... are you still there?"

"Oh, ah, yes, I'm here. No, no message, I guess. I'll just...try... again."

"All right then."

Dial tone.

# THIRTEEN

W hat we have to remember is that God isn't as interested in our circumstances as we are," Reverend Hughes said, "at least, not for the same reasons we are." He was smiling that odd little smile that Alexis found so engaging. She could never decide if he was listening to some inner joke or if he was trying to let the rest of them in on some jest that was slightly out of their line of vision.

"Now, I understand the temptation. After all, from the time we're kids in Sunday school, we're encouraged to put ourselves in the stories. I still remember sweet old Mrs. Clark and her flannel graph. We'd sit on the floor, cross-legged on our little carpet squares, and look up at her, and she'd tell us, 'Just imagine, boys and girls, if *you* walked out and saw a big, strong giant like Goliath frowning at you. And what if *you* were the little shepherd boy David, and all you had was five smooth stones, a sling, and a shepherd's staff? How would *you* feel?' She'd stick David up on the board, and he'd look like a young boy— like me or my best friend, Tommy, sitting next to me. And then she'd put Goliath on the board next to him, and he'd be a cross between Hulk Hogan and Captain Hook—with armor and a spear. It would get me every time. I'd spend the rest of story hour scared to death even though I knew David was going to come out on top."

Alexis smiled. She remembered the song she used to sing with her children: "One little stone went in the sling, the sling went around and around…" She couldn't remember the rest, except that at the end, the giant, naturally, came tumbling down.

"The thing is, when I read the Bible, I have to remember that the people aren't the point—not the people in the stories and not the people reading the stories. God is the point. Mrs. Clark didn't have a flannel-graph figure for God, but God was in every single story. Not only that, God was the main character, whether I realized it or not."

This bothered Alexis. Why would anyone create a being with self-knowledge and then expect it to become so thoroughly other-knowing? Even after nearly thirty years of marriage, she didn't think Brooks had known her. And, she had to admit, she probably hadn't known him either. And as far as God was concerned… Yet she found herself here in this pew, week after week, trying to find a way to God. Or trying to convince herself she was trying, as if failure to try was the only unforgivable sin.

She thought about the New Testament she kept in the top right drawer of her desk at work. She felt better just knowing it was there. But of what practical use was it? Did it make her kinder, more considerate, more patient, wiser? If she concentrated, she could probably quote most of Saint Paul's essay on love in the thirteenth chapter of the First Epistle to the Corinthians. Did that make her more loving?

"God's great at putting people in difficult situations to see how they'll shake out. And he's perfectly willing to work with whatever choices they make—even the bad ones," Reverend Hughes said. "God's not fussy. He'll take the lemons we give him and make lemonade—for us if we'll take it, but for somebody else if we won't. He sorts through the castoffs and the factory rejects and uses them to create beauty. He comes to the rummage sales we make of our lives and finds the bargains we've forgotten about. It seems to be a specialty of his. Don't ever count God out."

Eli closed his Bible, and the organist began playing the postlude. Alexis stayed very still in her seat as the other worshipers began moving toward the aisles and the back doors. She was thinking of a passage from C. S. Lewis. Was it from *Screwtape*? Something about the moment a human realizes, or at least believes, God has abandoned him but still chooses to cling to faith. What would make a person do that?

The greatest crisis Alexis had faced was her divorce, and she'd never really thought about blaming God for that. There was too much human fault in that situation to need a supernatural scapegoat. But what about someone in a different situation, someone who had kept to the straight and narrow and still got dealt a miserable hand? Why would such a person keep on believing when believing offered no apparent benefit?

With a minor jolt, Alexis realized she was falling into the precise trap Eli Hughes had just described. Maybe it wasn't about the sufferer after all. The conclusion seemed cold and unfeeling, but wasn't that still a consequence of taking the human point of view?

"But what other point of view am I supposed to take, for crying out loud?"

"Pardon?"

Alexis jerked her head upright and saw Reverend Hughes standing in the aisle beside her.

"Oh, Eli. I must have been deep in my woolgathering."

"Wonderful! It's nice to know somebody ponders the sermon once in a while. Uh, you were pondering my sermon, right? Please tell me you were."

She smiled at him. "Definitely."

"Oh, good. That's such a relief. May I?"

She scooted over, and he sat next to her. "Now, which of my brilliant points gave you such pause—if it isn't immodest to ask?"

"I was just trying to work out how it's possible to take anything other than my own consciousness as a starting point for my conclusions about God—or anything else. You said in your sermon that it's not about us really. But 'us' is all we know, isn't it? So how are you supposed to deal with something like…undeserved suffering, for instance? When you're in the bottom of the pit, it's pretty hard to take the heavenly perspective, wouldn't you agree?"

Eli shook his head. "I was hoping no one would ask that question." He looked at her. "You've smacked up against the biggest weakness in my case. Congratulations."

She tilted her head and gave him a confused look.

"Oh, don't worry. The church has been a going concern for a couple of millennia now; I don't think we're onto anything terribly revolutionary. But it *is* a problem. How are you supposed to get the Creator's take on anything when you're limited to being part of the creation?"

"That was my line, I believe."

The smile was back. "The problem of undeserved suffering has plagued the church since…before there was a church actually. Thing is, it's sort of hard nowadays to observe a truly righteous sufferer. Especially since Saint Augustine made original sin so popular and all."

"So you don't think it's possible for someone to have undeserved suffering?"

"No, I wouldn't go that far. I just said it's hard to observe. The Buddhists—now they're a different matter… What's wrong?"

She looked up at him. "Oh, nothing. I was just thinking of something. Someone, really."

He watched her for a few moments. "Something you need to talk about? Or someone, really?"

She gave him a faint smile and shook her head. "No. I just need to take God's point of view, I guess."

"Great answer. You get ten points for listening to the sermon." He stood up, still looking at her. "Sure you don't need to talk?"

"Not today. Sometime maybe."

"I'm here most days. Just call me anytime."

She nodded and stood. "Well…thanks."

"Anytime." He leaned toward her and gave her a quick hug. "From God. He said I should give it to you."

"Tell him I said 'thanks.' "

"Why don't you tell him yourself?"

She nodded and smiled, stepped into the aisle, and began walking away.

"Dr. Hartnett."

She turned. "Eli, how many times have I told you? 'Alexis.' "

He grimaced and smacked his forehead with the heel of his hand. "Sorry. But I have one final thought to leave you with. Or for you to leave with. Or whatever."

"Fire away."

"Just suppose that God really does love each of us as much as we've been led to believe. Leave the question of omnipotence aside for a second, and ask yourself how it must feel to love people that much and see them in pain—deserved or not."

She stared at him for several seconds, then turned and walked quickly away.

The tone buzzed in his ear a final time, then clicked over into Alexis's voice mail. "Hi. Sorry I missed your call. Leave a message, and I'll get back in touch."

Joe thumbed the End button and pocketed his cell phone. Too bad you couldn't hear the actual ring tone of the people you called. Hearing a person's ring tone told you things about him or her you couldn't learn otherwise. Alexis, for example. Did she have some utilitarian sound, like a bell or chimes or an ascending scale? Or did she use a Beatles tune maybe? And if so, which end of the continuum— "I Want to Hold Your Hand" or "Let It Be"?

Then there was her outgoing message: no name, no number. Just her voice, which she assumed you'd recognize if you meant to call her. Brilliantly efficient. More anonymous in one way, and more intimate in another.

Joe wondered if she was avoiding his calls. Of course she was. He'd just been laid off. He was under investigation. Why would any woman in her right mind, much less the one who was dean of his college, want anything to do with him? There was probably a healthy wager somewhere on who'd be the first to touch him with a ten-foot pole.

He really wanted to talk to her. Despite his best efforts to convince himself there was no point, he needed to know if she had written him off all her accounts. He felt sure if he could just see her face to face, he could tell her his story and make at least one person understand he wasn't a world-class screwup. Joe needed somebody to believe that, especially since it was getting harder and harder for him to believe it.

He touched the Mute button on his remote and leaned back into his couch. The TV evangelist was moving into her closing sequence.

"Now, folks, I can't tell you that everything in your lives is going to magically smooth out if you invite Jesus into your heart today. I can't tell you that your bills will be paid or your kids will start getting better grades or your dog'll quit chasing cars. But I can tell you this: Anything you have happening in your life right now will only be improved if you let the Lord come in. And nothing you're worried about is going to get any better if you keep him out."

Joe could never figure out why he watched this stuff. Was it the same instinct that caused young, impressionable children to be fascinated by scary movies? There was an element of Southern Gothic in this program; it reminded him of a Flannery O'Connor short story. The number for the prayer line crawled across the bottom of the screen as the bright, business-suited, middle-aged woman smiled at her studio audience and connected meaningfully with the cameras. The bumper sticker for this sermon could be something like "Try Jesus. What've You Got to Lose?"

He aimed the Off button at the television, and the screen went black. He got up and walked around the couch toward the front door. Outside, the sun was shining in that particularly heartening way that only winter sunlight possesses. He still hadn't become accustomed to the way weather swung back and forth in this part of the country:

freezing drizzle on Friday, followed by a Sunday afternoon that made you yearn for a pickup game of beach volleyball. He'd heard some of the faculty talking about the spring of two years ago. On Good Friday there was a foot of snow on the ground, they said, and on Easter Sunday the little kids were filling their egg baskets, dressed in shorts. How were you supposed to cope with seasons that wouldn't sit still?

His phone buzzed, a digital reproduction of the heavy black telephones of his childhood. "Hello?"

"Joe? You called a minute ago?"

"Oh, hi. Yeah, I guess I did, didn't I?" *Nice opening, Barnes.*

"Sorry I missed you. I turned my phone off during church and forgot to turn it back on."

"Oh, well, no problem. Say, I just wondered if maybe…that is, if you didn't already have lunch plans—"

"I'll pick you up in about five minutes."

"Is that a yes then?"

He thumbed the End button, leaned back into the cushions, and stared at the ceiling.

*Now, Barnes, what are you going to say to her?*

# FOURTEEN

Joe slid into the passenger seat and closed the door.

"What're you hungry for?" she said.

"Whatever the driver's hungry for."

"Tex-Mex?"

"My favorite comfort food after pot roast."

She smiled and eased out into traffic. "I'm glad you called."

"Really?"

"Yes. I've been wanting to talk to you about…things…and just haven't been sure how to start. Or when."

"I thought those were my lines."

She glanced at him. "Well, we're both exhibiting an appalling lack of initiative, it would seem."

"Better than having nothing in common."

"Oh, I don't think that's our problem."

He wasn't sure what to do with the silence that followed.

"Listen, Alexis, about this ethics investigation, I—"

"Joe, I want to tell you how much I enjoyed having dinner with you that night at Rizzuto's. It was a very special time."

He tilted his face and tried to regroup. She wanted to reminisce? But he was in the middle of his apologia.

"It was nice, yeah. Thanks for remembering."

She looked over at him, a trifle longer this time. "I've barely thought of anything else."

He still wore his confused look.

"Oh, dear," she said. "Now I've gone and shown my hand. I'm afraid it's been a little too long since I played the game."

"Game?"

"No, I didn't mean it like that. What I meant was…Joe, whatever happens, I think I know something about you that nobody can change my mind about."

"And…what might that be?"

She eased to a stop at a red light. She looked at him. "You're a good man."

Another pause while he tried to think of a suitably understated response. "Thanks, Alexis. That means more than you know."

They pulled into the parking lot and finally found an unoccupied space. The air was brisk but not unpleasant. Joe held the door for her, and they went inside. A warm, spicy draft greeted them, a wind from the kitchen laden with the green, red, and dusky tan aromas of cilantro, ground chili, and cumin. The undifferentiated swirl of voices swept over him, and Joe reflected on the many conversations going on:

146

whole families and tables full of friends who were blissfully unaware of trouble in the world or who were skillfully managing to ignore it, drowning it in a rising tide of *carne asada* and iced tea and *salsa verde* and talk. He envied them and mistrusted them, both at once. He was clearly in dire need of some good Tex-Mex and the hotter the better.

Alexis gave their names to the harried young woman at the hostess's podium, and they ducked past a hanging ristra of red peppers to find seats on a bench in the waiting area. The restaurant was full of people in Sunday clothes. Joe scooted next to Alexis and leaned against the wall.

"Popular place."

She nodded. "It's the buffet. Draws the AARP crowd every week."

"Ouch! I happen to like the buffet. And I expect to be a part of the AARP crowd before too much longer, I might add."

"Please, don't remind me."

"Surely an enlightened woman like you isn't hung up on the age thing?"

She gave him a deadpan stare. "Dear, at my age, it's hung on me, not the other way around."

Joe grinned at her. "Well, from where I sit, it looks like you're holding up just fine." *Oh, please! I think I used that line in junior high!*

She smiled and looked away.

"Dr. Hartnett, fancy meeting you here. And…Joe. How are you?"

Sophie Namath was standing in front of them. Her eyes flickered back and forth from Alexis to him; Joe could see her doing the equations in her head.

"Hi, Sophie," Alexis said. "I'd offer you a seat, but…"

"Oh, don't worry. I always forget how crowded this place gets at Sunday lunch. Guess if I went to church, I'd at least have somebody to eat with."

"Yes, that's a shame," Alexis said. "We've already told them there are two of us, and as crowded as it is—"

Joe silently offered thanks.

"Oh, don't worry about it, you two." Joe caught the ever-so-slight emphasis Sophie gave the last two words. "I'll just grab a chair in the bar. Tons of grading this afternoon. Gotta get back to it, you know?"

"Good to see you, Sophie," Alexis said.

Joe gave her a nod and a half wave as she swept past them toward the bar.

"Nice save," he said.

"I've known Sophie longer than you have," Alexis said. "Not to worry."

"You're the one who should worry. Being seen in a public place with the defendant. You sure your reputation's up to it?"

"Now that comment, Joe Barnes, was unnecessarily self-deprecating, bordering on needy."

"Needy? A guy who's out of a job in two weeks and facing an ethics investigation? What've I got to be needy about?"

"Not funny."

"Sorry."

The hostess called and led them back to their table. Alexis smiled and waved at several people along the way; Joe recognized none of them.

"I really am concerned about you," she said when they were seated. "How are you holding up?"

He shrugged. "I'm just trying to put one foot in front of the other, I guess."

Alexis looked at her menu and bit her lip. She looked like someone picking her way through a minefield.

"It's not that difficult, Alexis."

She looked at him, still biting her lip. "Why not?"

"Just get the buffet."

She rolled her eyes at the ceiling. "You just can't leave a moment alone, can you?"

"A good offense is the best defense, I always say."

"Well, you're probably right about the buffet. Shall we?"

They filled their plates with entrées of varying combustibility. When they got back to their table, a basket of corn chips and two glasses of iced tea were waiting. Joe tore a packet of artificial sweetener and emptied it into his glass, then pinched his lemon wedge and stirred. He took a long drink. "Ah...perfect. Am I the only person who resents it when the wait staff is too attentive? Like when you get your tea at just the right mix, and it's down maybe two inches in the glass, and they come and dump unsweetened tea on top of your carefully balanced blend? Please tell me I'm not the only person who hates that."

A smile flickered across her face, then straightened into a no-nonsense look. "Joe, I really want to know. How are you doing?"

He considered another offering of rapier wit but thought better of it.

"Oh, I don't know, Alexis. I'm…surviving, I guess. Just surviving."

"Is there anything I can do to help?"

There it was—and he didn't even have to fish for it. *How will I answer that question, I wonder?*

"I don't know, Alexis. I really don't know."

Her brow wrinkled; she leaned toward him. "I'm not sure I understand."

"Oh, I don't question your willingness or your intentions—nothing like that. It's just, well, I'm kind of tainted right now, wouldn't you say? I mean, how much can you really afford to aid and abet me?"

" 'Aid and abet.' Sounds like you've already court-martialed yourself and found yourself guilty."

Joe looked away, through the large plate-glass windows surrounding the quarry-tiled dining room. So much air outside, so much light. It was time for his flying fantasy to kick in. He could feel the cold wind on his face, smell the moisture in the clouds. He could look down and see the tiny buildings far, far below, past the tips of his toes. The wind would rush through his hair and between his fingers, dense and blue with altitude and speed. He would do barrel rolls and feel the un-obstructed sun on his face, his neck, his belly. He would forget; he would escape. Nobody could hurt you once you learned how to fly. You had no problems. Or if you did, you could put on a burst of speed and feel them tumbling off behind you, washed away in your slipstream.

"Aren't I?" he said, pulling his eyes away from the windows and back to her. "Just the accusation is enough for some people. Where there's smoke, there's fire, right?"

"Or a smoke screen."

"For what? I admit, the idea of a malevolent universe has always seemed to explain certain things, but why would anyone have it in for me? I haven't been here long enough to make enemies."

Alexis frowned at her plate, then stabbed at her enchilada. "I don't know, Joe. I'm just fishing, I guess." She chewed and swallowed. "Is there anything you might...want to tell me?"

"As my dean?"

She stared at him a long time. "Is that what you think this is about? I brought you to lunch so I could take some kind of deposition before you land in front of the ethics committee?"

"No, Alexis, I... That isn't it at all—"

"Because if that's what you're afraid of, we can get some to-go boxes right now. I'll drop you at your front door and set your mind at ease."

"Alexis, please, I'm sorry. I didn't mean anything like that."

They both stared at the tabletop for a long time.

"I'm sorry too," she said finally. "I guess I have more at stake here than I realized."

He looked a question at her. She reached for a tortilla chip and scooped a dollop of refried beans onto it. Without looking at him, she said, "After my divorce, I decided detachment was the safest way to live. And for quite a while it worked. I concentrated on my career and my kids and tried to make sure there wasn't room in my life for anything else. And then something happened that I hadn't planned for." She looked at him. "You showed up. And that pretty much fouled up my strategy."

He tried to think of something to say that could defuse the moment and realized he didn't want to. He waited.

"And so here you are and here I am, and both of us can tell what's starting to happen." She looked at him, and Joe thought she was a little afraid he might contradict her. He waited some more.

"And then everything starts to go haywire," she said.

"Yeah, haywire's a good word for it."

"I don't want to lose you, Joe."

He watched her eyes, afraid to look away.

"After all, I just found you. That would be a tragedy, don't you think?"

The moment stretched between them like a tightrope. Joe felt for his balance, knowing how easy it would be to tip one way or the other. He was sure there was no net.

"Alexis…God help me, how can I say this? What I feel for you is something I've never experienced before. It's precious to me—you're precious to me. And because of that, I'm afraid…of lots of things. Afraid for you and afraid for me. I don't know what to do with all of that, even if everything weren't…the way it is with me right now."

She slid her hand across the table and touched his fingertips. "I'll ask it again. How can I help you, Joe?"

He felt his own uselessness rising in his chest, trying to choke the words out of him that he couldn't say. *Call off the dogs! You're the dean—use the power. Make it all go away.*

No. It wouldn't do, and he knew it. If there was ever to be anything like real love between them, it had to stand or fall on its own merits, not because somebody had a magic wand.

He stared into her eyes. So deep and sad. What he really wanted at this moment was to never have to be without these eyes. Maybe she could see everything and still care for him. He didn't want to think about the alternative. Sometime, maybe soon, he was going to have to talk to her about…everything. But today he wasn't brave enough.

"What you can do for me, dearest lady, is…understand. No matter what happens, if I know somebody understands, I think I can make it."

She watched him, looking as if she was waiting for more. But he held himself still and sent toward her what he hoped was a small yet oh so sincere smile.

*Our decent yet stained hero keeps his silence, knowing that the merest slip of the tongue could compromise his true love in so many damaging ways…*

*Yeah, right. Move over, Dimmesdale.*

She drew back from him, but not, he dared to hope, in frustration or resignation. "All right then," she said. "You've got it."

"I do?"

She nodded. "Sure do." She looked at his plate. "And it's getting cold."

He grinned. "Now who's messing with the moment?"

She shrugged, dipping a chip into the picante sauce. "Learned from a master."

# FIFTEEN

May I remind you, Dr. Barnes, that the purpose of this inquiry is to complete some of the information in your personnel dossier. Regardless of your impending separation from the university, it's required that we thoroughly document all matters pertaining to your employment record up to this point. Is that understood?"

Lance peered down the table at Joe exactly as he would have if he'd been wearing bifocals, which he wasn't.

"Well, not exactly, Lance. I guess I'm still unclear on why this matter has anything to do with my employment—my present employment, that is. All this was investigated and dismissed at my previous university over twelve years ago—"

"Twelve years and eight months."

"What's the point of this exactly?"

Lance gave a pained look to the woman on his right. She was

roundish and tightly coiffed; she wore a severe navy suit and a bright red lipstick smile. The light glistening on her perfect teeth made Joe vaguely uncomfortable. Her eyes flickered toward Lance.

"That's a perfectly reasonable question, Dr. Barnes," she said. How could she speak without moving her lips? "No doubt your previous university intended to cover everything, but in going over the available records, we felt that certain matters were—how shall I put it?—glossed over. At least by the standards we use for such things."

"So, let me understand. Even though I was cleared of any wrongdoing, you aren't satisfied with the results?"

The red lips twitched, but she kept the smile jammed in place. "Well, I shouldn't put it *quite* like that, Dr. Barnes."

"How would you put it then, Ms., ah—"

"*Mrs.* Lawson. Mrs. Dorothea Lawson."

*Charmed, I'm sure.*

"I think we're wasting time here," Lance said, fingering the stack of papers in front of him. "The sooner we get started—"

"But I don't know if I want to get started. I just don't see how this can help anybody, and since I'm already fi— separated, it seems like a waste of time."

Lance gave him a half-lidded look. "Dr. Barnes, we have to complete your file. It matters."

"For what?"

"References for future employers. Professional accreditation. Processing your final paycheck."

Joe held up his hands. "Okay, fine. Let the lynching begin."

Mrs. Lawson's smile drooped ever so slightly. So her mouth did move after all.

Lance punched a button on the pocket cassette recorder at his left hand. "Now then. Dr. Barnes, perhaps you'd like to tell us how you came to know a certain student named..." Lance shifted the papers, peered at them. "Kim DiCarlo."

Despite himself, Joe closed his eyes. Kim. How had he *not* known her? And why hadn't he listened to himself sooner? Even after all this time, thinking of her was still like a jolt from a wall socket. Or... maybe not of her, exactly, but of what she'd represented to him back in that time so devoid of other signs of life.

"Ms. DiCarlo was enrolled in several of my courses at my previous teaching position."

"Yes...Survey of English Literature, Romantic Poetry, and..." *American Fiction Before 1900.*

"American Fiction Before 1900?"

"Yes, that's right."

"The last course was one you taught during your final semester. Is that right?"

"Correct."

"And it was during that semester that the, ah, events occurred?"

Joe nodded. He felt his stomach getting cold; his pulse was beginning to lope like a nervous colt. The thought of these two pawing through his past made him want to retch.

How could he ever hope to make anyone understand what he didn't fully understand himself?

❦

Kim DiCarlo was easily the most dedicated student in his Brit Lit class that first semester. Not the most talented, certainly; not even the most consistent in the quality of her work. But she cared about the meanings and the forms in a way that made Joe almost self-conscious about his lectures. There was an aching to know in her; it leaked from her eyes as she listened to him. Her voice was brittle with purpose when she read from *The Faerie Queene* or "Tintern Abbey." He admired her the way a teacher is supposed to admire a student who connects with the material. He genuinely looked forward to the days when he would see her in class.

But when she came back for Romantic Poetry, he soon realized that the connection might have to do with more than a mutual love of Byron, Keats, and Shelley.

What could he have done? He'd questioned himself a thousand times. Again and again he'd examined the way things had unfolded between them, trying to figure out where and why he'd permitted matters to cross an uncertain line. He was younger then: less able to carry the weight of fading dreams and an ailing marriage, less skilled at redirecting his attention from the lacks in his life. He hadn't then figured out that some voids weren't meant to be filled. At least by any method that was in his control.

She began to hang back after class to discuss some point of rhyme or meter or syntax. She permitted him slight glances past the lattice of what they were talking about into the courtyard of what she meant. Once, after a class reading and discussion of "La Belle Dame Sans Merci," she'd asked, half smiling, if he thought the Romantics were really in love with death or just with the images of themselves dying that they carried in their heads. "Well, for them, that would be pretty much the same thing," he'd said. "The Romantics were, by and large, much more interested in their imagination of a thing than in the thing itself."

She'd looked away, out the door, and said in a musing voice, "Can't really blame them. The world can be so…mundane."

"And reality can be so…real."

She'd cut her eyes at him then, realizing she'd been caught. "Touché," she said. And she smiled at him in a way that let him know she didn't mind, didn't mind at all. In that moment Joe knew he was in trouble. Wherever or whenever the line was, he'd crossed it.

$\mathcal{S}\!\mathcal{G}$

"Dr. Barnes, maybe you'd like to tell us in your own words the nature of the relationship between you and Ms. DiCarlo?" Mrs. Lawson said.

She was probably younger than Joe, but he couldn't imagine thinking of her any other way than "Mrs. Lawson." Maybe she was "Dorothea" to somebody, somewhere…maybe even "Dot." But he doubted it. He certainly didn't want to try to picture it.

"Ms. DiCarlo was a student—"

"Yes, we've established that," Lance said. Joe stared at him for several seconds, but he didn't flinch. Perhaps Lance had no notion of the border between efficiency and rudeness. Perhaps he was born without tact, the way albinos were born without pigmentation.

"…during a difficult time in my personal life," Joe said. "I was in the early stages of what proved to be divorce, and Ms. DiCarlo was…"

Mrs. Lawson leaned forward slightly with her elbows on the table. She was staring at him. *If she licks her lips, I'm outta here.*

"She was sympathetic, I guess would be the best way to put it. She was that way as a student, and she was that way as a…friend."

"And how did your, um, friendship begin?" Lance said. "Was it your idea or hers?"

⁂

Kim started walking with him. Often when he was headed across campus, she seemed to be headed the same way. After a while, he started to forget why it wasn't such a good idea. After another while, he started to look for her.

The first time they had coffee together, she looked straight at him with the same bearing-in gaze she used in class. "You aren't hiding the hurt from me, you know."

He asked her what she was talking about. He even managed a confused grin, thinking that might throw her off the scent.

"When you read 'Kubla Khan' today in class, the longing in your voice made me want to weep," she said, her eyes holding him like velvet talons.

He looked at her and knew he could do just about anything at that moment except lie. So he didn't say anything. He just kept looking at her until a waiter broke the trance by asking if they needed refills.

They came to think of it as their table, that little square of stylish chocolate brown laminate in the corner of the coffee bar. At first he had enough discipline to keep the conversation tilted in the general direction of Kim's hopes, dreams, disappointments, surmises, frustrations, and general theories. For a while that was enough: to listen to her and remember a time when he thought everything was possible and quite a few things permissible. He even managed to work in some fatherly wisdom just to maintain the plausibility of the illusion he was selling to himself with steadily decreasing success.

Loneliness plumed out of his pores like cheap perfume, and he knew it, and he knew she knew it. His vulnerability made him dangerous to them both, but he didn't have the strength to disengage.

"Ms. DiCarlo sometimes confided in me. At first I viewed it as a mentoring relationship—"

"What sort of confidences, Dr. Barnes?" Mrs. Lawson said.

"Oh, please. Nothing shocking or prurient. Just…daydreams really. Things she wished for. Things she remembered from her childhood."

Mrs. Lawson slid a glance toward her colleague, who made a notation on his legal pad.

"When did you first begin to suspect it was no longer a"—Lance consulted his notes—"a mentoring relationship?"

❧

The night she showed up at his front door, Joe was alone. It was that final semester; he was teaching pre–Civil War American Lit. Carol was on a consulting trip to the West Coast, and Joe was in that dreary no man's land between relief at her absence and guilt at his relief. He was listening to the Rachmaninoff *Vespers* and trying to finish an article for submission to the Modern Language Association journal. The doorbell rang, and he padded to the entryway in his sock feet, thinking it was another of the neighborhood kids selling Boy Scout popcorn or candles for the junior-high orchestra or some such thing. Joe was a bit annoyed, because the choir had just begun the *Nyne Otpushchayeshi,* the Russian Orthodox equivalent of the *Nunc Dimittis,* and the tenor was about to soar heavenward on the soft, pulsing updrafts of the St. Petersburg Boys Choir. Rehearsing his speech about having already bought from another kid, he pulled open the door and found himself staring straight into Kim DiCarlo's eyes.

"Aren't you going to ask me in?" she said, stepping over the threshold. Joe moved back, allowing the door to fall open, trying to remember if he'd said something, dropped some hint that his wife wasn't home tonight, praying he hadn't, but hoping he had. Kim's hand found the switch beside the door and swept over it, extinguishing the porch light as if by magic. The full moon was behind her, and she kept coming, reaching him, pressing herself against him, pulling his face toward hers. Rachmaninoff's tenor ascended, empowered and glorified, and Joe felt his heart, his mind, his spirit—everything he had—pouring out of him and into the welcoming softness of Kim DiCarlo's lips.

And then, for reasons that lay, as far as he could tell, somewhere between curse and grace, he pulled away from her. "No, Kim. No."

# SIXTEEN

S he looked at him. Her eyes were dark in the light oval of her face, staring at him out of a full moon as Rachmaninoff sighed for salvation in the background. He knew she wouldn't say she was sorry; she wasn't. He thought he was, but only because he knew how much they both had to lose.

He could hear his breath coming in urgent little puffs, fanning out into the silvery dark between them. He willed himself to slow down, to get a grip. He stepped around her and switched on the entryway light.

"Kim, there are so many things wrong with this I don't know where to start."

"Since when?"

"Well, for sure since about thirty seconds ago. And probably since before that."

She said nothing. She waited for him, watching him.

"There are codes of ethics, Kim, and this kind of stuff isn't on any of them."

That was when the hurt showed up in her face. " 'This kind of stuff'? You make it sound dirty."

"Kim, listen to me. I'm married—"

"To someone who doesn't treasure you one-tenth as much as I do. I can see it in your face, hear it in your voice—"

"And worse, I'm your teacher. I... This just can't happen."

"I'll drop your class."

Joe shook his head. "Kim, honey—" He grimaced. "Kim, listen."

He talked to her about every bad consequence he could think of. He told her that his firing would be the easiest thing to deal with, compared to the rest of it: the shame, the gossip, the ostracism from her peers, not to mention the likely strong disapproval of her parents.

"I'm twenty-three. I can even vote and buy beer."

He couldn't blame her for the sarcasm. Hell, after all, had no fury... But he wasn't scorning her. He was trying—admittedly, a bit too late and far too close to the edge of disaster—to rescue her. To rescue them both.

"Kim, let me tell you what's going to happen, okay? Tomorrow morning I'm going in to work a little early. I'm going to walk into the department chair's office, I'm going to close the door, and I'm going to tell Dr. Fisher that she needs to convene a professional misconduct committee to investigate me."

She stared at him as if a horn were sprouting from his forehead.

"If I don't call this on myself, somebody else might. And it'll be so much better coming from me."

"Who'd do that?"

"Somebody who saw us drinking coffee together every other day for the last month. Somebody who saw you in my office after class. Somebody whose nephew just finished his doctorate and is looking for a teaching position—I don't know, Kim. All I know is that this has to stop right now, and I have to stop it."

"But...I could make you happy."

"Nobody can make somebody else happy. All you can do, if you're lucky, is create a climate where happiness can grow if it wants to. And I'm afraid by the time we got through all the recrimination, embarrassment, negative consequences, and regrets, our little happiness garden would be just so much scorched earth."

Her eyes were beginning to shimmer. He knew a tear was about to fold gently over the rim of her lower eyelid, and he knew it would be as beautiful as a diamond, and he knew he would want more than anything in the world to brush it away with his fingertips. And because he knew all these things, when the tear started its run, he was adequately prepared to hold himself absolutely still and say nothing.

Her voice, when she spoke, was little more than a whisper. "Okay, okay. I get it. I think I knew things might go this way." She struggled gamely and came up with a quivery smile. "I'm pretty sure I hoped they wouldn't, but there you go."

He nodded and gave her a small grin. He jammed his hands into his pockets, hoping she hadn't seen his fingers twitching toward her.

"You're a good man, Joe—I mean, Dr. Barnes. And...I'll help you any way I can. With the committee, I mean. I'll tell them it was all my idea."

"No, I think these people could spot a lie like that a mile away."

She sniffed and ran the back of her hand under her nose. "Thanks for that, at least."

"Need a tissue?"

She shook her head.

"Good. I have no idea if we have any."

She let out a shaky laugh. "Okay. I'm going now."

"Thank you, Kim."

She turned toward the door. She stepped outside, then faced him. He gave her a shrug. She shrugged back at him. Then she was gone.

He didn't move until he heard her car start and saw her headlights backing down the driveway. When she drove off, he closed the door and leaned against it, throwing the deadbolt.

*If I've just done the right thing, why do I feel like crying my eyes out?*

꩜

"Ms. DiCarlo came to my house one evening and made...an advance."

"Did you encourage this advance?" Mrs. Lawson said.

Joe turned his head and stared away from them, into the blank space above the doorframe. It was the only place on the walls of the room not occupied by bookshelves stacked with vinyl binders. No books, just binders, and all black. They put Joe in mind of ranks of buzzards, glossy and patient, presiding from their perches over the events in the room below them. Joe wondered if the binders contained the statistical remains of Mrs. Lawson's previous victims. He wondered how long it would be before he was digested and encoded, housed like a cipher within the binders on the shelves.

After maybe ten seconds, he looked back at them. "The committee concluded I didn't. It should all be there in your report."

"We're interested in what you think, Dr. Barnes," Lance said.

Joe stared at the tabletop. He spoke without looking up. "If you want me to say that I had no desire for Ms. DiCarlo, that there weren't moments when I wished to be with her, that I never had any hope these feelings might be requited, then, yes, I encouraged her. If you're asking whether I did everything within my ability to prevent the relationship from progressing into a full-blown sexual affair, then, no, I didn't." He looked at them. "I did the best a flawed, lonely man could do in such a situation. That's all I can tell you."

Mrs. Lawson pressed her lips together and scribbled on her pad. She looked almost prim. Lance punched the Off button on the cassette recorder.

"Of course you realize, Dr. Barnes, that we'll need verification of your version of events."

"What do you mean? I thought you had the whole file from my previous employer. Everything I've said accords with—"

"Well, not exactly," Mrs. Lawson said, shooting Lance a look of frustration that he mirrored back to her. "We certainly made every effort to obtain all the pertinent documents. We contacted a"—she peered at her notes—"a Mrs. Hanks in your former department. This rather sketchy summary was all she could provide."

Joe offered a silent blessing for Beulah Hanks; she'd always tried to protect him. She was mad as a hornet when he resigned at the end of that year; she kept telling him he ought to fight all the way to the Supreme Court. Right now, though, he was wishing she'd been a little more cooperative; maybe they could've gotten this farce over with, once and for all.

"But what about HR? Surely you contacted them?"

"Their files were incomplete on this matter," Lance said, his upper lip curling in disdain. "We intend not to have the same outcome."

Joe shook his head. "What kind of corroboration do you require?"

"Do you have any idea how we might contact Ms. DiCarlo?" Lance said.

"Are you kidding? I don't even know if that's her name anymore. I haven't seen or talked to her in, let's see…twelve years and eight months."

Lance began stacking his notes. "Well, that's a shame, Dr. Barnes. Because until we can completely close this file, we won't be able to finalize your separation package."

"Or mail me my last paycheck."

Lance tucked the cassette recorder into the inside pocket of his tweed blazer. He didn't look at Joe.

"Dr. Barnes, this is standard procedure, I assure you," Mrs. Lawson said. "There's no personal agenda here."

Joe rolled his eyes and pushed himself away from the table. "So...what's next?"

Lance snapped shut his valise and stood. "If you can think of anything else you need to tell us that would help us complete the file—"

"Like locating Kim Whoever-She-Is-Now and convincing her of the importance of digging into ancient history."

Lance and Mrs. Lawson looked at each other. "Well, I think we're finished here for today, Dr. Barnes," he said.

Joe made a disgusted sound and walked out of the room.

Al went back to the parking lot. He made a beckoning gesture. Sophie and Bill got out of his car and came toward him.

"Okay, he's home. I can hear his stereo from twenty feet outside the closed door."

"You sure this is a good idea, Al?" Bill said. "If I were Joe, I'd probably want to be left alone." He was hugging himself and gazing longingly at the heated inside of Al's car.

"If you were Joe, you'd have already checked yourself into the stress unit by now," Sophie said. "Come on. Al's right; this is the least we can do."

The three of them walked toward the door of Joe's apartment: Al in front, Sophie second, and Bill bringing up the rear, still shaking his head and muttering to himself. They could hear the Eagles thumping out "Life in the Fast Lane."

"Not what I'd be listening to if my world was about to cave in on me," Bill said.

"See?" Sophie said.

Al rang the doorbell and got no response. "I've done this bit before. Joe! Hey! Come on!" He pounded the door with his fist. "Joe!" He pounded harder.

Sophie was peering through the window beside the door. "I can see his feet sticking off the end of his couch. No way he could be asleep though."

"What if he's…you know?"

Al gave Bill a disgusted look. "Bill, remember, this is Joe, not you. I'm sure he's fine…relatively speaking." He pounded harder.

"He's getting up," Sophie said. "Here he comes."

The door opened just as Joe Walsh began his rapid-fire guitar salvo leading into the final verse. It was like getting sprayed by a musical fire hose.

"Can we come in?" Al said.

"Huh?"

"I said, CAN WE COME IN?"

Joe nodded and stood aside as they filed into his apartment. He was wearing running shoes and warmups. He looked a bit puzzled as he watched them enter. Al tried to explain why they were there, but Schmit's bass and Walsh's guitar rode down his words like a steam-roller over day-old pizza. He made a dial-turning motion at Joe, who pointed a small remote at his stereo. The music faded to a slightly more conversational level.

"I don't get why you always play your music so loud," Al said.

"Please, Al," Sophie said. "You sound like my father."

"Sorry." Joe gave him a sad little grin. "Just trying to drive out the demons."

"Some demons," Bill muttered.

"Well, anyway," Al said. "We're here because, well, because we care about you, Joe. You've been through a lot lately. We just came by to…kind of…you know…"

"Watch you bleed," Sophie said. She saw Al's drop-dead look and covered her grin with one hand. "Sorry."

"Well, come in and sit down," Joe said, steering Al toward the couch. "I don't have much in the way of refreshments, but—"

"We don't need anything, Joe," Al said. "Just sit down and tell us how you're doing. Or anything else that's on your mind."

Joe pulled a wooden chair from beneath the counter of the kitch-enette and set it between the couch and the stereo cabinet, its back facing the couch. He straddled the seat and leaned his forearms against the back of the chair. He stared at them.

## SEVENTEEN

A l sensed everyone waiting for him to speak. "So, ah, you been exercising, Joe?"

"Oh, no…I thought I would when I got up this morning, but I just never got out and did it. Didn't really feel up to it, I guess. I turned on the stereo and just sort of vegged here on the couch."

Al nodded. Joe nodded. Bill and Sophie watched as if all this were fascinating and informative. In the background, the Eagles were singing about sunrises and ill-starred trysts.

"Well, um, how you doing?" Al said, wishing someone would help him bridge the gaping chasm in this communication process.

Joe shrugged. "I don't know, Al. I'm just kind of counting down the days, I guess, hoping something'll come through for me."

"How'd it go with the committee?" Sophie said.

Joe made a disgusted noise and shook his head. He stared above them, at nothing, as far as Al could tell. The Eagles sang about taking another shot of courage, and Al wished he had a drink in his hand. So what if it was before noon on a Saturday? At least it would give him something to stare into other than the lost expression on Joe Barnes's face.

"Look, you guys, I'm sorry. I'm just not a good candidate for cheering up if that's what you came to do," Joe said. "I'm running out of time and options. I thought getting back into teaching would be good for me, but…" He shook his head again.

"Joe, you're gonna beat this thing," Al said. "You're a good teacher; everybody knows that. And I'm sure there's no way the committee can make this investigation stick. When everything comes out, you'll be fine. You just gotta keep perspective. You just have to believe in yourself."

Joe looked at him, and Al knew his words sounded as weak to Joe as they had to him.

"Thanks for trying, Al," he said. "I appreciate it; I really do. It's just that the power of positive thinking hasn't worked out too well for me lately. You think I haven't tried? You think I haven't reframed and changed spins and looked on the bright side? Here's the thing, though: pretty much any way I look at it, it comes down to my being (a) barred from promotion, (b) fired, and (c) ethically and morally discredited. These are the facts in the case, as best I can see. Go ahead and remind me I've still got my health, if you want, but don't say it too loud, please. You never know who's listening."

Bill shifted uncomfortably. Al glared at him.

"Joe, have you thought about all your options?" Sophie asked.

He held out his hands toward her. "I've been thinking of nothing else, Sophie. I've sent out résumés, made phone calls—"

"No, I mean here. Options for this situation."

He looked a question at her.

"Do I have to spell it out? Have you talked to the dean? to Alexis? She can do something, Joe. She wants to. She cares about you."

Al and Bill looked at her, but she kept her eyes on Joe. From the set of her face, Al guessed she knew what she was talking about. She sure wasn't letting Joe off without an answer.

"That's not an option, Sophie," he said finally, looking away. "I can't put her in that position."

"What position? She's the dean. Her word carries weight. She can see what's going on here: one of her faculty is being put through the wringer for no good reason. Why don't you call her in?"

Joe wouldn't look at her. "Ex-faculty."

Sophie kept staring at him and began to nod slowly. "Okay. Okay, I see it now. The Last Good Man. Noble to the end, isn't that right? Taking one for the team, and the team couldn't care less."

"No, Sophie, it's not about that."

"Isn't it?"

"Sophie—," Al said.

"No, Al, let me talk. Alexis loves him. I've seen them together, and I've seen the way she looks at him."

"Uh, Sophie—"

"Quiet, Bill. I mean it; she loves him. And he loves her too, but don't expect him to admit it. He's too tightly wound around whatever deep, dark secret he's carrying to let anybody into the little heroic universe he's constructed for himself. Even someone who just wants to make him happy."

In the quiet that followed, "Tequila Sunrise" coasted in for a landing, and Don Henley and Glenn Frey started singing about what happens after the thrill is gone. It occurred to Al that when dreams did come true, they were, indeed, almost never quite like you planned. He wanted to give something to Joe, some kind of comfort. But at the same time, he realized he had very little to offer in the way of practical help, and what else could you expect after the thrill was gone?

And then, a little to his surprise, he started wondering what was wrong with Joe. Here was a guy who seemed to have everything going for him, and just like that, the whole shebang headed Dixie. Was Joe some kind of karmic lightning rod? Maybe he really had done something, sometime, to single himself out for the weirdly determined fate that seemed to be stalking him now. Disaster didn't just happen, did it? Al began to wish he were somewhere else; the things he was thinking were making him feel guilty and vulnerable.

He started to resent Joe for bringing him into contact with the soft underbelly of his existential consciousness. Maybe that was the center of it: somebody else's difficulties made you glad you dodged the bullet, then ashamed for being glad. Nobody really wanted to admit having the capacity for such crappy, self-serving ways of thinking. And mainly, nobody wanted to admit that something similar could happen to him.

Eventually, though, maybe you had to face the fact that all those differences between you and someone like Joe Barnes—the differences that were supposed to insulate you from misfortune—were mostly in your own mind. The screen between business as usual and life-altering mishap was tissue thin, if it existed at all.

"Okay, listen, Sophie," Joe said, rubbing his forehead like someone getting ready to explain quantum theory to third graders. "It's like this: twelve years ago when I was going through a very bad time in my... Why am I telling you this? What difference is it going to make anyway?"

"You never know until you try," Sophie said. She was sitting with her arms crossed and a go-ahead-make-my-day expression on her face. *Great*, Al thought. *As if Joe doesn't have enough trouble already.*

"Let's just say the committee wanted me to track down somebody I haven't seen in over twelve years and get her to document something that never happened. I told them everything I could, but they apparently don't think they have enough either to hang me outright or to let me off the hook."

"That actually sounds kind of interesting," Bill said, leaning forward on the couch. Sophie jabbed him with an elbow.

"In the meantime, they're holding my paycheck hostage until I can give them a smoking gun or an ironclad alibi." He shrugged. "What am I supposed to do?"

A few seconds crawled by.

"Well, if I were you, I'd try abject groveling," Bill said.

Joe gave him a weak smile. "Okay, that's honest advice."

"Not particularly helpful, but honest," Sophie said.

"Seriously," Bill said, "when you have nothing, you have nothing left to lose."

"When have you ever had nothing, Bill?" Al said.

"In reality? Not that often. In my deepest fears? All the time. I've fantasized more worst-case scenarios than the people at Homeland Security."

"I guess virtual reality beats no reality," Al said.

Bill shrugged. "I call 'em as I see 'em."

"Franz Kafka meets *The Cat in the Hat*," Sophie said.

"I hate to admit this," Al said after a moment, "but I kind of agree with Sophie. *And* Bill."

"No kidding?" Bill said.

"Maybe you should talk to Alexis. What have you got to lose?"

Joe sat very still. Staring into the middle distance, he said, "More than I'm willing to risk."

Sophie flung her hands into the air. "Joe, honestly! What are you talking about?"

"You can't love a lifeboat, Sophie. You can't love a parachute."

She looked at Joe a few seconds. "Can anybody love a pariah? Because that's what you'll be when the committee gets finished, if you don't do something."

"I don't know yet," he said. "I guess maybe I'm going to find out."

Bill looked from Joe to Sophie. Then he looked at Al. "You catching any of this?"

"I think so," Al said. "Check with me later."

"Don't care about winning, but you don't wanna lose," the Eagles sang, "after the thrill is gone…" Al had a sudden, intense desire to be out of here before "Hotel California" started. He stood. "Well, I guess we should get going, guys. Leave Joe to his weekend."

"Since our work here is done and all," Sophie said.

"Thanks for coming, you guys," Joe said. "Really. I know why you did it, and I'm grateful."

"I'm clueless," Bill said.

"And that's different how?" Sophie said.

"Well, no matter how all this turns out, Joe, I, um, I wish you the best."

"Thanks, Al."

"I wish you'd reconsider," Sophie said.

"I wish somebody would tell me what's going on," Bill said.

Al opened the door, waiting for Sophie and Bill to catch up with him.

"Well, good-bye," Joe said. "I guess I'll see you around."

Al nodded, looking toward his car. He felt as if he were standing in front of the White House and had just found out the missiles were on the way. But he couldn't admit that to anyone. So he stared longingly at his car and wished Sophie and Bill would please, please hurry a little bit.

✍

Alexis stared out her window. The day hung low and gray like tattered drapes. Hovering above the tops of the trees in her yard, a dark blue, bruised line of clouds moved toward her, promising weather even more dreary than the clinging, damp chill now beading her windows with condensation. Maybe a storm was coming. Wouldn't that be just great? Maybe it would be better afterward, like tying the string from your loose tooth to the doorknob and actually being able to make yourself slam the door hard enough to remove the nagging misery from your mouth.

But there were storms, and then there were storms. A summer rain shower left everything fresh: colors more vivid, the air rinsed clean, the dust settled. It broke the grip of the heat and reminded you that relief was possible. And then there were the violent thunderstorms, complete with barrages of hail that broke windows, punched holes in roofs, and left new cars looking like victims of bat-wielding vandals. There were tornadoes that turned whole subdivisions into facsimiles of London during the Blitz. Hurricanes that drowned entire sections of coastland. Blizzards that roared in with a blinding white howl, stranding drivers and leaving the corpses of wildlife beneath a frozen shroud. A storm wasn't always a gift.

She stared at the paper in her hand, a copy of the memo Lucy had sent to the Human Resources office. She'd been carrying it around with her for the past week and a half; it was creased and scuffed from riding in her purse with her makeup, her wallet, her keys. Lucy's spiteful little accusation had taken up residence among Alexis's essential items, moved in with the stuff she kept with her at all times. She would no more throw it away now than she would toss her pocket-sized packet of Kleenex.

When she first saw the memo—after marching down to HR, cornering some poor student worker, and bullying her into opening the file—her impulse had been to rip it into pieces and fire Lucy on the spot. She hadn't done either. She was still trying to figure out why.

Maybe it had something to do with the way Joe had reacted that day at lunch. She had practically invited him to have her weigh in, and he'd declined. Why?

Alexis hoped it was because he knew what a fragile, shy thing love could be. She hoped he knew that at certain stages, love was vulnerable to a host of parasites and predators, one of the most malevolent of which was the suspicion of being wanted for something besides oneself. There were so many ways to use people, ways to replace them in your heart with the things you wanted them to do for you. It could happen without your knowing it.

Alexis stared out her window; the clouds huddled closer.

# EIGHTEEN

L ucy heard Alexis's heels clicking down the hallway. She stared at her computer screen and braced herself for the icy blast. Alexis strode into the office, passed Lucy's desk without a glance, went into her office, and closed the door behind her.

The cursor blinked on Lucy's screen. It wasn't as if she hadn't prepared to accept the consequences of her actions. She'd been ready for anything: an angry lecture, a transfer to another department even. But in some ways, the cold silence was worse. It left her alone with her thoughts, forced her to go over her actions again and again, examining her motives like a forensic scientist looking for clues.

She'd done the right thing, hadn't she? Didn't predators rely on the silence of their victims and the passive complicity of their peers? Wasn't that how Polly had wound up in her situation?

She recalled a conversation she'd had with Polly about one of the courses she'd taken last semester. It was a class on the physiology of aging, and Polly had told her that on one of the exams, the answer to nearly every question involved the phrase "shrinks and loses elasticity." It seemed funny at the time.

Lucy stared at the backs of her hands. The liver spots were getting more pronounced. She faithfully slathered on every new product touted by the youth merchants, but the skin on her knuckles was still taking on the dry, scaly appearance of elephants' knees. Her hands were turning into her mother's hands.

She remembered a time in elementary school when her brother—the little boy who would one day become Polly's father—got in trouble. Lucy was in the fifth grade; Carl was in the third. A boy in Carl's class had accused him of stealing his lunch money to buy candy. When Mother confronted him, Carl stoutly denied everything.

Lucy knew the boy; he was just the spiteful type to make a false accusation for no reason other than getting somebody else in trouble, but when Carl tried to tell Mother, she wouldn't listen. She was wearing that look she'd adopted after Daddy left: the look that said she didn't need a faithless husband around to raise her children, thank you very much, and no lying son of hers was going to get the best of her.

Lucy's heart sank as Carl dug in his heels and Mother's demands for a confession became more and more strident. They were both trying to win, but *nobody* was going to win. Lucy stared at Carl, pleading with her eyes for him to just give Mother what she wanted, but he clamped his jaw shut and said nothing. They both knew they were right, and neither was going to admit defeat.

She wanted to run to the little bedroom she shared with Carl in their small apartment. She wanted to crawl into her bed and hide her ears in the pillows and be nowhere until this was over. Instead, she followed in horrified fascination as Mother yanked Carl down the hall to the apartment's tiny, green-tiled bathroom.

Mother grabbed the thick, scarred, brown strip of leather from the nail behind the door. She bent Carl over the commode and swung the strap three times. Lucy could see little puffs of dust flying up from Carl's elastic-waisted dungarees as the razor strop thwacked across his backside. Each time she hit him, he scrunched his eyes and gritted his teeth, but he didn't make a sound.

"Are you ready to tell me the truth?" Mother said, breathing a little hard.

"I already did," Carl said through his clenched jaws.

Mother jerked him upright and started unbuttoning his pants. Lucy ran into the bathroom and grabbed her mother's hands, wrapping her own arms around Mother's.

"Mother, stop it! Stop it! Carl's telling you the truth. Just don't hit him anymore." She wept in deep, shuddering sobs, sickened to her stomach by the need of her mother and brother to punish each other for nothing more than being who they were.

Being right wasn't enough sometimes, was it?

Lucy took a deep breath and closed her eyes for a minute. Things would work out somehow. They always did.

She started typing again, wondering if your heart could shrink and lose its elasticity.

*✑*

Joe drove the number-two pencil around and around in smaller and smaller rings until the tiny circle was completely black and shiny. He set the pencil down and flexed his fingers and wrist. He couldn't understand why they had to submit grades online and with a hard copy too. Even though this was the last official task he would perform as a professor, he was glad it was over. He slid the grade master into an interdepartmental envelope and wound the string closure around the tabs. He was about to walk down the hall to the English office when he saw the corner of a clear report cover with black comb binding protruding from a stack of papers at the corner of his desk. It was his Thomson fellowship proposal. He slid it out and began to flip through the pages.

> *Henry James has written that Hawthorne judged "the old Puritan moral sense, the consciousness of sin and hell, of the fearful nature of our responsibilities and the savage character of our Taskmaster...[from] the point of view of entertainment and irony..."*[17]
>
> *Some might even suggest that Hawthorne paints his progenitors in dark tones only that he might distance himself from them...*
>
> *And yet, one also finds traces of something more in Hawthorne's professed attitudes about his theological and*

cultural genealogy. In "The Snow-Image" from Twice-Told Tales, Hawthorne writes:

> ...[N]or, it may be, have we even yet thrown off all the unfavorable influences which, among many good ones, were bequeathed to us by our Puritan forefathers. Let us thank God for having given us such ancestors; and let each successive generation thank him, not less fervently, for being one step further from them in the march of ages.[18]

If Hawthorne means to do nothing more with the darker aspects of early Puritan society than use it as a negative advertisement for the advantages of more modern social and religious theory, why does one so often find his characters engaged in a vain struggle to escape their own guilt—or, at least, its consequences?

Is it too difficult to wonder if Hawthorne's gratitude for the increasing distance between himself and his spiritual forerunners is driven by more than allegiance to the thought of his contemporaries? Or is some deeper, less congenial motivation at work in him? Is it possible, in fact, that Hawthorne's artistic enterprise is, at least in part, an attempt to reconcile himself with those facets of his own nature that stand judged by the austere mores of his ancestors?

Joe closed the cover. He wondered if the words he'd written would sound as self-serving to everyone else as they did to him at this moment. Surely Gwen Kenton's project, whatever it was, would make a much more attractive entry in the Thomson catalog than his dubious quest for the alleged skeletons in Nathaniel Hawthorne's familial closet.

Wasn't it Garrison Keillor who said, "Guilt is the gift that keeps on giving"? Maybe that was the best thing about someone else's guilt, real or imagined: it was a handy distraction from your own. Maybe Job's friends were only doing what anybody else would've done under the same circumstances.

There was a quiet tap at his doorframe. Joe spun around to see a short, square man. He had the crew cut, blocky look, and the thick hands of a longshoreman or perhaps an Olympic weightlifter, but the clerical collar around his neck indicated a slightly different career path.

"Hi. I'm Eli Hughes. You must be Dr. Barnes. Alexis told me I might find you here."

Joe pushed himself out of his chair and held out a hand. "Hi, Reverend Hughes. Sorry I didn't hear you walk up, but please, come in." Joe scooped an armload of books off the only other chair in his office.

"Actually, I prefer 'Eli,'" the minister said, sidling around the corner of Joe's desk.

"Well, I prefer 'Joe,' as long as it's between friends."

"I sure hope so." Eli sat. His black Hush Puppies barely reached the floor, and for some reason, Joe found this oddly comforting. He had a black woolen overcoat draped over his arm, and he tossed it casually on the floor. He gave Joe a friendly smile.

"So, ah, Eli, what brings you around?" Joe said once he'd decided Eli was waiting for him to speak.

"Well, I'm not really sure. All I know is that I got a call from one of the folks at my church, Alexis Hartnett—whom you know?"

Joe nodded.

"She said she'd like me to talk to someone. I said sure, and she gave me your name and told me I'd probably find you here, working on your grades. And...that's about it."

Joe felt a confused look wrinkling his face. "That's it?"

Eli nodded.

"Do you often answer such cryptic summons from your parishioners?"

"Actually, not nearly often enough. Back in seminary, I had all these romantic visions about getting those urgent calls in the middle of the night, you know? Maybe it's got something to do with my name."

"Maybe if they'd named you Samuel instead..."

Eli grinned and shrugged. "Maybe so. But by the time I'd been in ministry a couple of years, I figured out that being a preacher can be fairly routine. Boring, even—though I don't admit that too often."

"Well, I guess I never thought of it from that angle."

Eli nodded. "Alexis's call was intriguing, to tell you the truth. Enough so that I guess I sort of forgot to press her for details."

Joe stared at him for a few seconds, and Eli returned an open, interested look that said he had all day if that was what they needed. It didn't seem he planned to hurry the process by asking questions, nor did he appear to be the type who needed to chink the silences with small talk. As far as Joe could tell, Eli Hughes was content to be exactly where he was, doing exactly what he was doing. At some other time, Joe might have found this impression admirable. Under the present circumstances, he found it a bit disconcerting.

"I'm feeling at a bit of a disadvantage here."

"How so?"

"Well, you have to admit, this is a pretty odd situation."

"Two guys being introduced by a mutual friend?"

"Well, no, not that part, exactly. But...don't you feel as if you've been sent on a mission?"

"Sure I do. But what's odd about that? We're all on a mission of some kind, aren't we?"

"And you have no curiosity at all about why you're here?"

"Certainly. Tons. But that doesn't give me the right to pry."

Joe gave him another puzzled look.

"Here's the thing, Joe. Alexis knows you, and she knows me. For some reason, she cares enough about you to ask me to come, and she also respects you enough to give you total control over what I know or don't know. The ball's in your court. You wanna tell me to take a hike? Tell me to take a hike."

Joe tried to imagine himself ordering this fireplug of a man to do anything he didn't want to do. The picture was comical, a bit like the bookish kid with the skinny arms trying to shove a Greco-Roman wrestler out of the ring.

"Honestly, this is the last place I want to be if you don't want me here," Eli said. "But if you have something you'd like to get off your chest—and I think maybe you do—I have nothing else I'd rather do than listen. It's totally up to you, Joe."

Eli sat back and crossed his arms. He was still looking at Joe with that patient, engaged expression. The silence stretched taut as Joe tried to decide what to do.

# NINETEEN

O kay. You said you had a feeling I needed to talk. What gives you that idea?"

Eli gave an embarrassed grin and ducked his head. "How can I explain this? I get a sense, sometimes, about people. Like when they're pretending to be different than they really are—happier, or more secure, or wealthier, or smarter, or more interested in religion. I get that one a lot."

"And your alarm went off when you saw me?"

Eli spread his hands. "I prefer to think of it more as a spiritual gift. Call it a divine smoke detector."

"So which category do you have me pegged in?"

Eli looked at him. "Happier," he said. "I see somebody who's doing his dead-level best not to let on that his world is falling down around his ears."

Joe puffed out his cheeks. This conversation had clearly reached its Rubicon. He realized he was thinking more of Alexis than he was of the man sitting across from him. What was going through her mind when she dispatched this cherubic muscleman on his mission of mercy? Had she sent Eli Hughes to him because she had nothing else to give?

Eli was right; Alexis had left him the dignity of choice. Joe was under no obligation—not even that of acknowledging his need for a pastoral visit. Joe felt a sudden surge of affection for Alexis. It occurred to him that it took a great deal of trust to give this much leeway to someone you cared about.

Joe gave Eli Hughes a long, careful look. "If you're really interested in hearing this, we have to start at the beginning."

Eli smiled. " 'In the beginning…' Three of my favorite words."

"My world wasn't exactly without form and void, but it was getting that way in a hurry."

Joe told him about the long, grinding misery of watching his marriage die and not knowing what to do about it. He told him about Kim DiCarlo, about all the places she'd touched in him that he'd thought were dead. He told Eli of their close encounter and his strategic retreat to the relative safety of the Manhattan publishing world. He told of the nagging, inconvenient love of teaching that had lured him here. And he told about the failure of his Thomson proposal, the downsizing, and the current stalled investigation.

"I guess that pretty much brings us up to today," Joe said.

"Wow. So you've lost your academic momentum, your job, and now possibly your reputation. I would say you've still got your health, but that usually doesn't play too well here."

"Not so much. I've already warned my friends off from using it."

Eli took a deep breath and let it out slowly. "This is a tough one." He looked at Joe. "What do you think you're going to do now?"

"I thought you might have a suggestion. Aren't you in the advice business?"

"Who, me? No, you have me confused with the astrology column."

"Your candor is refreshing. So...no deus ex machina to bring this little drama to a happy ending?"

"Well, in my line of work, I've learned never to count out intervention from unexpected sources. Of course, the thing that's so blasted frustrating about that is it's so...unexpected. Makes it hard to plan for. And darned near impossible to control."

Joe nodded. "Yeah. They don't really cover prayer in *What Color Is Your Parachute?* do they?" He tried to smile but couldn't quite manage it.

Eli peered at him. "What?"

Joe shook his head. "Nothing really." He rubbed his jaw and looked away. He knew without looking that Eli's eyes were fixed on him.

"Your alarm going off again?"

Eli waited.

Joe fidgeted with the corners of his Thomson proposal. "Well, it's just... I mean, does it seem right to you that we find ourselves in these predicaments, not all of our own making, and are left to fend mostly for ourselves?"

Eli waited some more.

"Is it too much to expect help every now and then?"

"What kind of help are you wishing for?"

To his surprise, Joe felt a tiny surge of anger somewhere deep in the center of his forehead. "You really want to know? Any kind, Eli. Anything would be better than the cosmic silence I get when I try to…"

"Pray?"

"Not really. Just…make sense of things, more like. Prayer seems to already assume too much somehow."

"What do you think you're asking for, Joe?" Eli said. His voice was like someone reaching toward Joe with kid gloves. "What do you think you really want? Really."

Joe stared at his proposal folder. The words were upside down, angled away from him. He looked up at Eli. "A hearing. I want a hearing."

Eli nodded slowly. "Well. Maybe you'll get one, Joe." He grabbed his overcoat from the floor, then stood and began edging around Joe's desk. "I think I'm about done here for now. You don't have time to waste on messengers with no message."

"I'm sorry, Eli. I didn't mean to offend."

"You didn't. I'll take honesty any day of the week, no matter what else it's packaged with. You'd be surprised how little of it I run into."

"That's worth something then, I guess," Joe said. He stuck out a hand, and Eli shook it.

"Okay, this will probably sound pretty hypocritical now, but…if you don't mind, toss up the odd prayer for me, will you?"

"Guaranteed." Eli shrugged into his overcoat and walked away from Joe, down the hallway, then turned. "Odd prayers are my specialty."

He gave Joe a little wave and kept walking. He had a wide, side-to-side kind of walk, this cinder block of a man who stretched the seams of his overcoat taut across his shoulders. Joe watched him leave, wondering how much wrestlers and saints had in common and why.

*✑*

"How am I supposed to find her?"

"Well, you managed to locate Dr. Barnes's former department. I'd suggest starting there."

"Even if I am able to somehow track down this woman, how do we know she'll talk to me?"

"I'll deal with that when and if you document my need to do it," Alexis said. "But in the meantime, it's absolutely in your best interest to locate Kim DiCarlo and very, very politely request her assistance in this matter. Do I make myself clear?"

Lucy donned the tight-lipped, prim expression that told Alexis she was thinking things she couldn't say. Fine. But if Lucy thought Alexis was backing down on this, she'd soon learn otherwise.

Alexis stared at Lucy until she jabbed the mouse on her keyboard. When she saw the splash screen for Lucy's address book program, she turned and closed the door to her office, hoping Lucy hadn't seen the smile starting across her face.

Alexis sat at her desk and swiveled to look out the window. Sleet spattered the panes. The campus was almost deserted, especially since the winter storm warning had squalled from the radios. In a way, the warning was responsible for her tête-à-tête with Lucy. When Lucy had come in after the National Weather Service notice, asking to go home, Alexis decided in that instant: no, not only would Lucy not go home, but she would stay here and at least attempt to untangle the snare she'd constructed for Joe Barnes. Clarity. Just like that.

This felt right. No more waiting to see, no more soul-searching over motives and outcomes. She was dean of this college. Why shouldn't she decide when she'd intervene and when she wouldn't? Let the chips fall where they might.

The wind moaned past her windows and launched a fresh fusillade of sleet. *Let it blow,* she thought. *The harder, the better.*

The phone buzzed in her ear once, twice. *Good,* Lucy thought. *Maybe no one will answer.* But on the third ring there was a click and a voice on the line.

"English department."

Lucy winced. Of course the Hanks woman would be at her desk today of all days. Didn't she ever take any time off?

"Hello, Mrs. Hanks. I don't know if you remember me or not, but a few weeks ago I visited with you about turnover patterns among tenured faculty—"

"You're the woman who was trying to dig up dirt on Joe Barnes. Sorry, not interested." Dial tone.

Lucy closed her eyes and took a deep breath. Glancing at Alexis's door, she pressed the Redial button on her phone.

"English department."

"Mrs. Hanks, please listen to me. I…I need your help."

"With what?"

"Our HR department is trying complete the file on Dr. Barnes, and there are certain…gaps in the record."

"I thought maybe if I made it hard enough for them, they'd just give up and do something that might actually help somebody. But they decided to go ahead, huh? I guess some people actually enjoy digging into other people's trash heaps."

"Now, Mrs. Hanks, it isn't—"

"Yes, it is, honey. That's exactly what this is, and why you decided to pick on Joe Barnes is beyond me."

"Mrs. Hanks, there was nothing personal—"

"Don't even go there. I've lived too long and seen too much not to know a nasty little vendetta when I see one."

"There's really no need for—"

"Sure there is. I'm an old woman, and if I don't vent my spleen every so often, I get really cranky. And then I might decide not to give you what you're looking for. Like the phone number on this little piece of paper I have here on my desk."

There were several seconds of silence as Lucy tried to think how to speak to this infuriating woman. "Mrs. Hanks, we very much need to speak to a Ms. Kim DiCarlo."

"Yes, I'll bet you do. But what are you going to do when she tells you to take a flying leap, as she has every right to do?"

"If I could just have her contact information, I won't trouble you anymore."

"Now, there's a promise worth considering. Okay, tell you what. I'll give you her number on one condition."

Lucy tried to wait her out, but she clearly wasn't budging. "What condition is that, Mrs. Hanks?" she said finally, doing her best to keep her voice level.

"That when Joe Barnes is exonerated—and he will be, if I have to come down there and personally read the riot act to everyone in sight—you'll have him call and inform me. Dr. Barnes and no one else. Otherwise, I will come to your campus and track you down. Capisce?"

"Yes, Mrs. Hanks. I quite understand. Now…may I please have the number?"

She read the number, and Lucy copied it down. Mrs. Hanks made her read it back. "I don't want to have to talk to you again because you transposed something," she said. Lucy bit her lip, then read the number back.

"Okay then," Mrs. Hanks said. "I'd wish you luck, but I don't really mean that, except for Joe Barnes's sake." And then she hung up.

Lucy had to get up from her desk and pace for a few minutes, trying to regain a portion of her composure. Half a dozen times she started to go into Alexis's office and threaten...something. Half a dozen times she thought better of it.

When she could feel the muscles in the back of her neck starting to relax, she went back to her desk. She looked at the ten-digit number that would lead her to Kim DiCarlo. She took three slow, deep breaths, then picked up her phone and began dialing.

# TWENTY

Joe inched along the street, as close to the curb as he could get without scraping his tires. His wipers wagged back and forth in front of him, screeing across the icy windshield like twin metronomes from hell, but the sleet caked onto his windshield faster than the blades could remove it. His headlights cast a meager, unsteady beam into the swirling storm. He cursed himself for not taking the money out of his dwindling savings account to repair his heater fan; he could see his breath misting in front of his face.

Just when he thought his shoulders would snap from the tension, his headlights found the apartment parking lot. He crept through the maneuver, turning his steering wheel with the exaggerated, two-fisted caution of an octogenarian making her weekly drive to church. The parking lot was full of ice-coated vehicles owned by people too prudent to venture out in such a blizzard; he had to park a good two hundred feet from his apartment. He got out and closed his car door, then tried to lock it, but the keyhole was scabbed over with sleet. Joe decided that any car thief working tonight would probably freeze to death anyway. He picked his way across the parking lot.

When he got inside, he reached into his pocket and looked at his cell phone. It had rung while he was driving, but with the treacherous conditions, he was too afraid to take a hand off the wheel long enough to dig it from his coat. He thumbed the button to display the missed call.

*Alexis.*

Joe tried to imagine the conversation they would've had if he'd answered his phone. He stared at the numbers on the tiny blue screen, trying to divine from their shape and spacing whether good news or bad would follow his pressing of the Return Call button.

He realized he was still wearing his coat, that he stood in the middle of his living room staring at the phone in his hand. He also realized that his door had just blown open with a gust of freezing wind because when he saw Alexis's number, he'd forgotten to shove it closed behind him.

*Just call her. What can it hurt?*

He tossed his coat across the back of the couch and leaned against the door until the latch clicked. Sleet pecked at the windows. He walked around the couch and perched on the arm, still staring at his phone. He closed his eyes, punched the button, and put the phone to his ear.

"Hello?"

"Hi, Alexis. You tried to call me?"

"Joe." A long pause. "I have to talk to you."

"Okay. Before I forget, though, thanks for sending Eli around."

"Oh. He found you?"

"Sure did. We talked."

"How'd it go?"

"Good. But you should probably ask his opinion too."

"Honestly, I care more about yours."

"Really?"

"Really. Joe…I read the transcript of your meeting with the conduct committee, as well as the background files from your previous school. I know about Kim DiCarlo."

Another long pause. "And?"

"Can I come see you?"

"Now? Alexis, the streets are dangerous—"

"Yes, I know. I'm afraid to drive home actually."

"Where are you?"

"In your parking lot."

"You're kidding."

"Not even a little bit."

"Umm…sure, come on in. I'll put on some coffee."

Just as he emptied the carafe into the coffee maker, the door blew open, and Alexis blew in. He closed it behind her and held out his hands for her coat, but instead she pulled him to her and wrapped her arms around him.

"Nice to see you too," he said into her shoulder.

She held him away from her and looked at him. "I knew I was right about you."

"You did? How?"

He held her coat as she slid her arms out. "It feels so good to get off the fence and do something about all this," she said.

"Do what about what?"

She looked at him. "Joe, you don't have to worry. I know why you were evasive, and I know why you wouldn't ask for my help. I understand. And it's wonderful."

"It is? What is?"

She went to the kitchenette and looked at the coffee maker. The water was just starting to trickle through, barely stained by the freshly ground Colombian Special Roast in the filter compartment. "Looks like we have a while to wait here. Aren't you going to ask me to sit down?"

On her way to the couch, she paused at the entertainment center and ran a finger down the CD stacks.

"Hmm, I don't see any Barry White here." She turned and smiled at him.

"And that's…a good thing?"

She came over to him and put a hand on his cheek. "For now, yes. Later…we'll see."

Joe's pulse bumped up from a brisk walk to a slow jog. She took his hand and pulled him toward the couch. "Come on. I have things to tell you."

She sat facing him, still holding his hands. "Do you know the biggest fear I had in all this time, since your...problems started?"

"That I'd turn out to be the predatory scum HR apparently thinks I am?"

She shook her head. "I really don't like it when you talk about yourself that way."

"Sorry."

"I was afraid that... I'm almost ashamed to admit this."

He stroked the back of her hand with his thumb.

"I was afraid you'd ask me to bail you out. And if I didn't or couldn't..."

Joe nodded. "I understand. Believe me."

"But you didn't, Joe! You didn't! You took everything they threw at you, and you never brought me into it. Do you know what that means?"

"That I have absolutely no future as a politician?"

"Will you stop it? I'm being serious here."

"Sorry again."

"It means, my dear Dr. Barnes, that you are in love with me, not with what I can do for you."

He looked at her, and the quip on his tongue evaporated in the glow of her eyes. "I believe you may be right," he said.

For a second he thought she was going to lean toward him, but she blinked and looked away, toward the kitchenette. "You think there's enough coffee in the carafe for two mugs?"

He looked over his shoulder. "Maybe." He got up and went to the cabinet. There were exactly two mugs in something resembling a clean condition. "I'm not sure if I have any cream or anything."

"I'll take it black if it's good coffee."

He gave her a hurt look. "Hey, I'm an English professor. Or was. You think I'd serve you preground?"

"Sorry."

He came back to the couch and handed her a mug. She raised it toward her and inhaled, and something about the angle of her face and neck, her eyes closed in appreciation of the coffee's aroma, made Joe want to touch her. Instead, he sat down and took a careful sip. "So…pardon me for looking a gift horse in the mouth, but I'm not quite clear why it's okay for you to get involved now when it wasn't before."

"Simple. Because I don't have to."

"Come again?"

"If I had to, I couldn't. But I don't, so I can. See?"

"Not…so much."

"Never mind then. Just know that some things are about to change for the better."

"Okay."

They sipped their coffee and listened to the wind yowling outside.

"I talked to her," Alexis said.

Joe did his best to keep his face absolutely still. "You did?"

"Today. Just before I left my office. That was why I had to see you."

Alexis had imagined all sorts of voices for Kim DiCarlo, and each carried its own prefabricated persona: the husky alto of a temptress like Kathleen Turner or Lauren Bacall; the fluting birdsong of an ingénue in the mold of a young Audrey Hepburn. She might even evoke the world-weariness of Marlene Dietrich or Kristin Scott Thomas in *Four Weddings and a Funeral;* Alexis could easily imagine Joe being attracted to the sort of intellect that was too old for its years.

And so, of course, when Kim's voice actually came on the line, Alexis was completely surprised. She sounded like the prototypical suburban woman. If Alexis had been in charge of casting the voices for a radio commercial for household products or a new children's clothing store, she would have chosen the voice that was speaking in her ear.

"Hello? Is someone there?"

"Oh, I'm sorry," Alexis said, grabbing for the note Lucy had scribbled just before forwarding the call to Alexis's phone. "Am I speaking to Kim...DiCarlo?"

"Well, it hasn't been 'DiCarlo' for several years now. But you have the right person. I'm still confused about why you've called though."

"Yes, Kim, I can guess this must seem strange after all these years."

"It has something to do with Dr. Barnes? Joe Barnes?"

Alexis contemplated the sound of Joe's name coming from Kim's lips. She let her mind sift it for a moment, trying to decide if she could detect any residue of the emotions Joe had once, presumably, aroused in the woman on the other end of the line.

"Kim—may I ask your last name, please?"

"Oh, sure. It's DeVry." There was a little laugh. "Like the technical institute."

"I think you're a university now."

"Oh, really? Well, that's a step up, I guess. It was sort of handy, not having to change my initials."

Alexis put a smile in her voice. "Mrs. DeVry—"

"Oh, dear. Was it something I said?"

"Sorry. Kim, then. Kim, did my assistant give you any background on why we've contacted you?"

"She told me it had something to do with Joe's—with Dr. Barnes's personnel records at your university. But what's that got to do with me?"

As gingerly as she could, Alexis told her. She told Kim about the investigation, and she was proud of herself for not pronouncing the word with quotation marks around it. She spoke of the need—again, no quotation marks—of the HR department to know as much as they could about the nature of Joe's relationship with her, the relationship that had prompted the original inquiry and Joe's subsequent change of careers.

Alexis finished talking and waited, listening to the white noise on the telephone line as if it was auditory tea leaves that might help her divine the thoughts running through Kim's head. The pause passed the point of a quick dismissal. It was too late for "Oh, that was so long ago, and I was just a crazy kid with a crush." The silence was moving on toward something more substantial, something Alexis wasn't sure she wanted to hear. But she waited, schooling herself to patience as the woman at the other end of the call, the other end of Joe's life, gathered herself to say whatever she was going to say.

"I suppose I should be angry or insulted." Kim said finally.

"That possibility had entered my mind," Alexis said.

"It's odd though. As I think back on that time, I only remember good things."

Alexis waited.

"First, you must of course know that Joe Barnes is a complete gentleman. His behavior toward me was appropriate in every way."

Alexis let out a long breath she hadn't realized she was holding. "I'm glad to hear that, Kim, but I'm certainly not surprised."

"If anyone crossed the line, I did. Oh, I suppose he could've been a little more circumspect about letting his vulnerability show, but then again, that's part of what makes him a great teacher. Or did, as I remember."

"I agree."

"The thing is—excuse me, what did you say your name was?"

"Alexis."

"The thing is, Alexis, loving Joe Barnes as I did was really what enabled me to release him and myself. It was the best kind of love, the kind that respects the other's freedom too much to compromise it, certainly too much to put him in any sort of jeopardy. Once he helped me see the consequences, there was only one loving thing to do: step back. And that decision—which Joe helped me make, in the most considerate and respectful way—set the course for the rest of my life. I wouldn't have any of the good things I have now—my husband, my kids, my career—if Joe hadn't been the kind of man he is. Does any of that make sense?"

Alexis was nodding. "Yes," she said. Her voice was a little fogged over by what she was feeling; she cleared her throat and assumed her best imitation of a businesslike tone. "So, to be clear for the purposes of this call, Kim, it's your assertion that Joe Barnes did not at any time behave improperly toward you, as a student?"

"That's what I'm saying. I'm saying a lot more than that, but I'm definitely saying that."

"Well, I want to thank you, Kim, for speaking to me. You were certainly under no obligation to do so, but you've cleared up a great many questions, and I think we can put this business to rest now, once and for all."

"I'm glad. Will you do one thing for me, Alexis?"

"Of course."

Kim gave her the message, saying Joe would understand its meaning, and Alexis didn't doubt for an instant that he would. And for a brief moment, she was jealous of even this moment of remembered connection. "Of course I will, Kim. I'll tell him those exact words."

# TWENTY-ONE

A sudden blast of sleet rattled the windows like a handful of bird shot. Alexis had been silent for a long time. Joe was looking at her, waiting for her to tell him about the conversation with Kim. And to hear the message Kim had confided to her. He wanted to ask her, to nudge the moment along. But even more, he wanted to trust Alexis to shape what came next.

Alexis looked at him. "She said I should tell you, 'Hester has made her peace. And so should you, if you haven't already.'"

Joe felt the words barrel into his mind, his heart. It was as if Kim were sitting here with him, telling him herself. For a couple of seconds, time and distance evaporated, melted away by the remembered connection between two hearts. He realized he was smiling. And then he remembered Alexis and understood what it had cost her to deliver the message.

"Alexis, you don't have to—"

"Worry? I'm not worried, Joe. Not about you anyway."

She closed her eyes and tilted her chin, and this time Joe started to lean in, when Alexis abruptly stood.

"The campus will probably be closed tomorrow because of the ice. But as soon as the streets start to clear, I want to see you in my office. From there, we'll go down to Human Resources and get this ridiculous situation resolved."

Joe started to remind her that the streets were treacherous and wouldn't she rather just wait it out here, with him? He started to tell her that even when HR was satisfied, or exorcised, or whatever the term was, he was still out of work. He started to tell her that, notwithstanding all that, everything in the world would be just fine if she would only sit back down and keep looking at him as she had just after she had finished talking about Kim. But all he said was "Okay."

She gave him a quick, businesslike nod. "Now, where is my coat?"

He got it and held it for her as she slid into it. "Thank you." She turned to face him as she buttoned it. "And now, I have to make a little confession."

His heart started its expectant lope again.

"I wasn't quite truthful with you earlier," she said.

"How so?"

"Actually, I'm not at all afraid to drive home."

His look begged for more information.

"During the winters here, I always carry tire chains in my trunk. I'm quite resourceful, you see."

"How could I have ever doubted that?" Joe said.

"So I could've gone home quite easily. Except for one thing."

He waited.

"I really had to see you." She leaned in quickly, kissing him and brushing his cheek with her fingertips. "And now I absolutely must go before I compromise my administrative impartiality any further."

"But...hold on a second! I hear administrative impartiality isn't all it's cracked up to be."

She smiled, and the look in her eyes was worth at least five publication credits. "Nice try, Dr. Barnes. See you soon."

She went out. Joe leaned against the doorframe and softly pounded his forehead against the closed door.

*≪≫*

The sun came out the next morning, and by early afternoon rivulets of water were running down the gutters as Joe drove up to the campus. Sure enough, there were several cars in the parking lot, including Alexis's.

He walked into the dean's suite. Lucy looked up when he came in and smiled at him but not before he detected something else in her face chagrin? embarrassment? or just frustration?

"Dean Hartnett's expecting you, Dr. Barnes."

No mistaking it: Lucy had a stiffness in her voice that told him she had something stuck in her craw. *Throat,* he corrected himself.

Alexis hung up the phone as he entered her office. "Joe! I just spoke with the director of HR, and the committee members are on their way up right now to meet with us."

"On their way from where?"

"Doesn't matter. They needed a little persuading, which I was only too happy to provide." He grimaced. She smiled sweetly at him. "Not to worry, Dr. Barnes. You've been under the microscope long enough. It's someone else's turn."

"It's always someone's turn, I guess."

"Well, in this case, they really do have it coming, in my opinion."

A very audible sniff came from outside.

"Why don't I close the door?" Joe said.

Alexis shrugged. "If you want. Makes no difference."

Joe closed the door quietly and sat back down. Alexis was looking at him. They locked eyes for a moment, until he felt the need to disengage.

"So…I guess maybe I have a shot at getting my last paycheck anyway?"

Alexis looked down at her hands, folded on her desk. "Much less than what you deserve, but, yes, at least that." A few seconds slid past. "Joe, maybe we can find something for you at one of the community colleges around here. And I know some people in administration with the public schools. Maybe—"

"I won't have to move? Maybe not, Alexis." He realized he'd never before used her first name in this office. "I don't want to go anywhere else."

Her eyes were on him again, and this time he didn't look away. Not for a long time. After a while she closed her eyes.

Her phone chirruped. She pressed a button. "Yes?"

"They're ready for you in HR."

"Thank you, Lucy." She stood and gave him a bright, expectant look. "Shall we?"

"Why not?" He stood and held out a hand to her. She took his hand and gave it a little squeeze. She picked up a manila folder from her desktop, then strode to the door and pulled it open, gesturing him through. Joe was pretty sure Lucy didn't look up from her computer screen as they went out.

When they opened the glass doors leading into the Human Resources offices, a nervous-looking student worker was standing in the waiting area, watching for them.

"Right this way, Dean Hartnett. Mr. Simmons and the committee are waiting for you in the conference room."

"The director of HR is meeting with us?" Joe whispered as they walked down the hall.

"At my explicit request," Alexis said, smiling serenely and looking straight ahead.

As they neared the conference room, Sophie Namath exited a door farther down the hall. She walked toward them, hesitated slightly when she saw them approaching, then gave Alexis a beaming smile and stuck out her hand.

"Dr. Hartnett, Dr. Barnes. Good to see you."

Joe nodded. "And you, Sophie," Alexis said. "What brings you to HR?"

"Oh, just…a little cleanup work, I guess. Well, gotta run." She gave them another shiny smile and walked away briskly.

"She's everywhere you want to be," Joe said under his breath.

Alexis jabbed him with her elbow. "Not by a long shot, Dr. Barnes. And here we are."

He had to suppress a shudder of uncomfortable familiarity when the student worker ushered them into the conference room. He looked around at the bookshelves; the binders were still here and didn't appear to have been consulted or otherwise disturbed. In an attempt to break the jangling of bad karma, he took a chair on the opposite side of the table from where he'd sat previously. Alexis put her hand on the back of the chair next to his and started to pull it away from the table, but then she pushed it back in. She took the seat at the opposite end of the table from that occupied by the director of Human Resources.

Jim Simmons looked none too happy, but compared to Lance and Mrs. Lawson, flanking him, he looked like a kid at a carnival. Lance had the disgruntled air and slightly disoriented look of someone who'd been waked from a winter afternoon nap, and Mrs. Lawson's bright red lipstick was noticeably missing. Joe wondered exactly what sort of persuasion Alexis had used to get them up here on an errand he doubted they were relishing.

"Thank you for coming, Lance and Dorothea," Alexis said. "And,

Jim, I appreciate the arrangements you made in order to join us." She smiled at the trio at the other end of the table as if she'd just complimented their grandchildren; they stared back as if she'd just informed them of a pending IRS audit. "As you know, there are some outstanding matters concerning one of my faculty, Dr. Barnes here, and I've come into possession of information that I believe will allow us all to close this matter and move on to more important things."

Lance's jaw muscles began flexing in and out. Joe ordered himself not to smile. *Not out of the woods yet…*

"The HR department's ethics committee was requiring confirmation of certain matters related to Dr. Barnes's last teaching position." Alexis placed on the table in front of her the manila folder she'd brought from her office. She opened it and studied the first couple of pages, then closed it. "Lance, I think you'll find in here everything you need to close your file." She picked up the folder and held it toward the other end of the table. After a few seconds, Lance pushed himself up from his chair and moved the bare minimum steps required to take the folder and return to his seat. The three of them looked at each other, then at Alexis. She returned their gazes with a calm, patient expression that looked as likely to budge as an oak stump.

Lance gave a resigned sigh and opened the folder. He read for a minute or so, then pushed the file toward Mrs. Lawson.

"Jim, as you'll see, I have an authenticated transcript of a telephone conversation with the young woman mentioned in Dr. Barnes's records. As you can also see, she was quite forthcoming in her admiration for Dr. Barnes, both then and now. She was most definite on the matter of the propriety of Dr. Barnes's behavior. Quite a remarkable conversation, actually, considering how long ago the events actually occurred."

Mrs. Lawson's eyes flickered toward Alexis. She smiled with all the warmth of a pit bull and returned to leafing through the document.

"In addition to this transcript, signed by me, I also have a recording of the conversation, which I made with the subject's permission. You can listen to it if you like."

Jim Simmons shifted in his chair. "That won't be necessary, Dr. Hartnett. Mrs. Lawson, may I?" He reached over and slid the folder from in front of Mrs. Lawson. He opened the cover and gave it a cursory glance. "Lance, Dorothea, any reason why we can't get this finished up?"

"Today?" Alexis said.

Lance and Mrs. Lawson looked at each other a few seconds. "I suppose not," Lance said finally. "We'll need copies for the HR files, of course."

"That's yours there." Alexis said. "I've already made copies for myself, and I'm giving the originals to Dr. Barnes."

"Sure, fine."

"And when can Dr. Barnes expect his financial arrangements to be completed?"

"Payroll cuts in two weeks," Mrs. Lawson said.

"Surely Dr. Barnes won't have to wait so long. After all, as the transcript shows, none of this should have involved him in the first place. Wouldn't you agree, Jim?"

Jim Simmons made an impatient face. "I guess we can expedite the check. Anything we can do to be helpful."

"Wonderful. Well, does anybody have any questions? If not, I'll just have my assistant send around a memo that summarizes everything." Alexis was still smiling; Joe contemplated how much he would hate to be sitting on the HR end of the table today.

# TWENTY-TWO

Well, I guess I'll head over to my office and start boxing things up." Joe and Alexis walked back toward the administration building. At a place where the building shaded the sidewalk, a patch of ice still held out against the rising temperature. "Watch it," he said, grabbing her elbow. "That's still frozen."

"Thanks," she said, taking his hand as she stepped around the ice. "It's melting though."

Joe looked around. Alexis was right; everything he saw was evidence of the thaw. After the bleak charcoal gray backdrop of yesterday's storm, today's sunlight seemed to have some sort of positive mass. Its tendrils pressed beneath everything frozen, lifting with delicate, irresistible force. As Joe watched, slender needles and larger, tree limb–molded tubes of ice slipped, losing their fingernail hold on the sycamores and elms, and fell rattling to the ground as harmless as cocktail cubes. Every naked tree was an impromptu fountain; every downspout clattered with the news that the freeze couldn't hang on any longer.

"We've still got some winter left," he said. "This time of year it always comes back."

"But days like this are still good for something," Alexis said. "I know I need them."

She hadn't bothered to remove her hand from his. Joe tried to sense everything he could about Alexis's palm, her fingers. He tried to make himself conscious of every square inch of the places where their skin touched. There were so many ways to hold a hand. What a huge difference there was between holding a child's hand to cross a busy street and sharing a touch with a beloved. One was unilateral, protective, and often proprietary. The other could be that too but was so much sweeter when it wasn't—when the desire to be touching was mutual and open ended, when you knew that at any moment the other person could choose to withdraw from your touch but at every moment she was choosing not to. Joe wished he could send all the warmth in his body into his palm, into the gentle curve of his fingers where her fingers nestled. They walked that way until they reached the door of the administration building.

"See you later?" she said.

"Count on it."

She went inside, and Joe turned toward his building, walking with his hands in his pockets and wondering why he felt so much like smiling when he was about to be unemployed.

He had now packed up three offices in his professional life. Three offices, two apartments, and roughly half of one very nice three-three-two with lots of extras and just over twenty grand in equity—his part anyway.

He thought about Nathaniel Hawthorne on the day he was finally able to bid farewell to the hated city of Salem and the job of port surveyor by which he'd eked out a living for three years. He'd been fired too, come to think of it; this was long before the notion of downsizing. What had the brooding artist carried out of his offices in the Port of Salem, along with his personal effects? Resentment, certainly. Probably at least a little guilt over whatever had led to his firing. His Puritan heritage primed him for remorse; he surely wouldn't have completely squandered such a fair-and-square opportunity. And, Joe guessed, he'd carried with him a dose or two of self-doubt: Hawthorne, after all, had burned the unsold majority of his first books.

Whatever he took, he'd loaded it and his family into a wagon or buggy and carted it with him back to Concord, where he'd salted it down, deep down in his thoughts, tamped it tight with a plug of native New England taciturnity, and allowed it to ferment with the grief over his doting mother's death. True, after the publication of *The Scarlet Letter,* followed by the election of his friend Franklin Pierce as president of the United States, circumstances improved for his household. But still, how long had Hawthorne kept some of those old, dusty crates packed up, secreted in some dark corner? How long had he carted them from place to place in his mind, bemoaning their weight yet unable or, worse, unwilling to leave them by the side of the road?

Why, Joe wondered, did so many people hold on to stuff long after its usefulness had ended?

*Thank you, Kim. And thank you, Alexis.*

Joe decided to clean off his shelves before foraging for boxes. Feeling a sudden burst of energy, he took the steps into his building two at a time, nearly colliding with a worried-looking Al Tielman.

"Whoa! Sorry, Al. Guess I need to look where I'm going."

Tielman gave him a dismissive wave and started past. Then he stopped and looked at Joe.

"Actually, we need to talk. You got a minute?"

"You kidding? I have nothing but minutes, remember? I was just on the way to start cleaning out my office."

"Yeah... Yeah..."

Joe gave Al an odd look, but Al didn't appear to notice. In fact, he seemed to be having some sort of inner dialogue for which Joe's presence wasn't necessary. Al grabbed Joe's elbow and pulled him through the doorway back into the building.

"Yeah," he was saying, "Why not? This ought to work. No reason why it shouldn't. I can't imagine the dean having a problem with it, and even the provost knows we have to cover the load..."

Joe started to ask Al to include him in the discussion, but since Al seemed to be making such good progress on his own, Joe decided not to interrupt.

They were getting close to Al's office. Leaning against the wall outside, like Edith Piaf standing beneath a streetlight, was Sophie Namath. She had her arms crossed in front of her, and she was shaking her head and smiling.

"I guess he figured it out," she said.

"Who?" Joe said.

She nodded at Al. "It took him a little longer than I figured, but I guess he finally got there."

If Al had any idea anyone was speaking, he gave no sign. He motioned Joe through the doorway, still scratching his chin and mumbling to himself like someone trying to solve a quadratic equation in his head.

"Good luck, Joe," Sophie said, leaning through the doorway. "Everybody knows you deserve it."

Joe gave her a puzzled look just before Al tugged him into his office and closed the door.

"We have a problem, Joe, and I think you're the solution," Al said before he was in his chair.

Joe gave him a surprised look. "That'd be a switch."

"Sophie just resigned."

"Excuse me?"

"Yeah. Said she had an offer she couldn't refuse, starting in January. Said with the stuff going on around here, she didn't think she much wanted to hang around anyway. She's already been to HR for her exit interview. Without talking to her department chair first!"

"Shame on her."

"So... Next semester she was scheduled to teach Women's Lit Before 1900, a section of Shakespeare, and two sections of freshman comp and lit. I have less than three weeks to cover her courses. You interested?"

"You're kidding, right? This is some kind of practical joke you and Bill cooked up?"

"I'm serious as a heart attack, Joe. I have until the middle of January to get somebody ready to teach Sophie's classes, and I don't see why I'd want to shop around when I have somebody of your caliber already here."

"Don't you want to check with HR to make sure I'm not a sexual-harassment risk?"

Al looked like he'd just swallowed a piece of bad sushi.

"I forgot about that."

Joe shrugged. It made him a tiny bit ashamed to realize how much he was enjoying this. Knowledge really was power. "Maybe you should check with the dean," he said, managing to keep a straight face.

Al stared at him for maybe five seconds, then grabbed his phone. He punched in a number; Joe heard the muted buzzing through the back of the earpiece.

"Lucy? This is Al Tielman. Is Alexis available? Yeah. Okay, thanks."

Al picked up a pen and was doodling nervously on his desk blotter: squares which he crosshatched and then recrosshatched at the opposite angle. They followed each other across the blotter like tiny, box-shaped elephants in a circus parade. When he was halfway through shading his fifth box, Joe heard a click in the earpiece.

"Alexis? Yeah, it's Al. Listen, I have a situation over here. Well, yeah. Sophie Namath just tendered her resignation. No, I'm not kidding. Yep. Just like that. Said she had a…what? Well, he's here right now actually. Sure, sure. Of course. Yes, that was my thinking also, and I want to, but I need to know if the…"

Joe carefully kept his eyes directed elsewhere as the sound of Alexis's voice, loud even from where he was sitting, took center stage in the room. Al sat, nodding every now and then, even grimacing once or twice. Joe estimated it was at least two minutes before he managed to interject even a symbolic "Uh-huh."

"Well, of course I always suspected that," he said after another thirty seconds or so. "Sure. I'm glad to hear it. No, that's okay. I understand. It's been hard for all of us. Okay. So we're good to go? Okay. All right. Thanks, Alexis. Yeah. You too."

He placed the phone in its cradle and gave a low whistle. "That is one ticked-off lady."

"So…what's the verdict?"

"Acquitted of all charges, sounds like to me," Al said, leaning back in his chair and giving Joe an expansive smile. "So, whaddya say? You want to hang around with Bill and me another semester or two? It'll be a little dull with Sophie gone and all, but at least our boccie team would stay intact."

Joe did his best imitation of someone carefully weighing alternatives. He managed to hold the attitude for a good ten seconds before the grin broke its traces and stampeded across his face. "Sure. When can I pick up copies of Sophie's syllabi?"

*Guess I don't need those boxes after all.*

Lucy dipped her spoon into the steaming broth, stirred it slowly for a few seconds, then lifted it. She tilted the spoon and watched the noodles and small, brownish cubes of chicken cascade back into the plastic foam cup, watched the golden flecks of chicken stock tumble in slow motion, churned by the turbulence of the tiny cataract.

She'd failed to tell Dean Hartnett she was taking her lunch break. Oh, well.

As soon as Al Tielman's voice came on the line, she'd known. It seemed so inevitable. Alexis's tirade had then confirmed it: Joe Barnes was staying on. He had won the day. The whole year, more like.

Lucy wondered what qualities made certain people immune to harm and others so apparently destined for it. Why did some people ride the crest of every wave while other desperate dog paddlers spent every moment trying not to drown?

She told herself the observation wasn't motivated by jealousy. What did Joe Barnes have for her to be jealous of? She wasn't in competition with him; her only interest was the welfare of her boss and the academic enterprise for which she was responsible. She had no personal agenda.

She lifted the spoon to her mouth, blew carefully across the soup, and took a cautious sip. The broth was still hot; it nearly scalded her tongue before she could take a quick sip of water to cool it down. She wished she hadn't forgotten her bowl; it was wide enough to allow the soup to cool to an edible temperature. The cups from the faculty-staff commons were great if you wanted to eat your lunch on the polar icecap.

She took another sip of water to cool her tongue. Someone came through the door behind her; she didn't turn her head. Lucy heard footsteps heading toward the kitchenette, heard the microwave door open and close, heard the beep of the number pad, then the whirring of the oven. The oven whistled, the door opened, and the person left.

Lucy stirred her soup and tried to figure out where she'd gone wrong. Not just with Joe Barnes. She thought about the fierce happiness in Alexis's voice as she talked to Al Tielman: the joy of someone who'd won a hard victory in a just cause. She imagined the relief Alexis was feeling—and Al Tielman too, probably. No doubt the whole university was throwing one big party to celebrate the vindication of Saint Joe the Unjustly Accused. Lucy wondered, if the roles had been reversed, if anyone would've cared as much about her vindication.

She tried another sip from her cup. She blew on it a little longer this time and was able to swallow without scorching her soft palate. This pup tent of self-pity she'd zipped around herself was a threadbare sort of comfort. There was probably a better, more constructive way to go, and one day soon Lucy would likely search for it. But not yet. Not today.

She took another dip with her spoon, blew on it, and reached gingerly forward with her lips.

# TWENTY-THREE

A lexis went to tell Lucy to e-mail HR and notify them of Joe Barnes's rehiring, but Lucy wasn't there. Alexis glanced at her watch. A little early for lunch, but…

She felt a nudge of guilt, realizing she had been enjoying the prospect of having Lucy transmit the instructions. Maybe it was just as well she had taken an early lunch. Alexis wrote the e-mail herself.

After clicking Send, she wheeled about in her chair to look out at the sunlit winterscape. The scene reminded her of Hawthorne's short story "The Snow-Image." The children in that story had fashioned from the winter-heaped snow a beautiful, perfect—yet ultimately perishable—playmate. She thought about how yesterday's storm, by coating everything with the treachery of ice, had set the stage for today's glistening tableau; the sound of dripping water reminded her of blood returning to numbed fingers, of drought-ending rains in summer. The glad, sun-spawned ruckus chattered life and the ultimate coming of spring.

But Joe's words were nagging at her. It was still winter. The calendar on her desk blotter stated the dour and obvious fact that spring lay on the far side of at least two and a half more months of possibilities for worse weather than yesterday's. The world was defrosting, but it wasn't going to last.

Alexis felt the beginning of panic, a cold spot in the center of her chest that was trying to work its way to her brain through the base of her skull. She wanted to find Joe. She wanted to go somewhere with him right now—a place of forgetting or maybe of starting over.

Wasn't there a time when she'd felt every bit as exhilarated in Brooks's presence as she now did in Joe Barnes's? Hadn't they started their marriage in a blushing, heated rush of solemn promises and giddy anticipation, as much in love as two people thought they could be? Alexis didn't have to try hard to remember the days when forever seemed far too short a time to enjoy everything with her husband that she wanted to enjoy. Those days were on the far rim of a chasm of dashed hopes, disappointments, grim secrets, and cumulative betrayals...but they had existed.

Yes, there was still plenty of winter left. There would be more freezes, more foul weather. The sun would go behind a cloud. Gold would dim to a sullen gray, and then where might comfort be found?

Alexis studied the bleak terrain of her failed marriage. Where had they gotten off track? When had they stopped delighting in each other and started enduring each other? The process was so gradual, so daily. She'd often wished for some major event, some watershed—

something she could point to and say, "Here's where we went afoul. Just stay away from this place, and everything will be fine."

But there wasn't such a place. As in Millay's poem, love had left Alexis and Brooks in little ways. As the verse said so well, the very imperceptibility of the process was part of what made it so disheartening.

Alexis stood and grabbed her coat. Cinching the belt around her waist, she strode out of her office and down the hall. She descended the nearest stairway and found the closest door.

She walked in the brisk, laundered air, swinging her arms like a cross-country skier, as if fending off invisible pests. Her heels tapped the sidewalk, a decisive one-two cadence that carried her across the quadrangle at the center of the oldest part of the university. She reached the gate and made a sharp right turn, headed down the street that fronted the campus. Traffic hissed past her on the wet streets. She walked with fists clenched and eyes straight ahead, the picture of determined purpose. Too bad she didn't know where she was going.

To be going—maybe that was the thing. She certainly felt better sensing the blood accelerating through her veins; the contact of her soles against the pavement, steady as a heartbeat; the weight of her swinging arms. Yes. She had to keep going.

She teased at the thought some more, tried to get a fingernail under the edge of the notion that she wanted to pry loose.

What connected anyone to anyone or anything else? Love, probably. No...definitely. Love was what made hope possible, and faith.

Love of one sort or another—perhaps even in its perverted, selfish forms—supplied the energy that fueled every decision, every action, every idea. Maybe it was what powered the cosmos. That was what people like Eli Hughes seemed to think.

What if she was onto something? What if love was the thing that connected you with eternity? If it did, then it was at once the most precious thing in the universe and the most dangerous. It was a two-edged sword, capable of cleaving soul and spirit, joint and marrow.

*Ask yourself how it feels to love your creation that much and see it in pain—deserved or not.*

Maybe the worst thing you could do with love was waste it, no matter the risk. There was such a thing as too much safety. Maybe love was more important than information. Maybe it was more important than answers.

At this thought, she stopped, right there on the sidewalk. She looked around and realized she was in front of the coffee shop where she'd seen Joe the first time, waiting patiently for his order, too decent to frown at the hapless cashier making him late for his class.

She thrust her hands into her coat pockets and stared at the plate glass of the windows, seeing herself as a dim reflection in the foreground, cars blurring past in the background. She smiled. She closed her eyes for a few seconds, bowed her face toward the sidewalk. Then she turned and walked back the way she'd come: slower now and with a greater calm than she could remember feeling in quite some time.

"Okay, don't forget that your poetry responses are due next week," Joe said to the accompaniment of slamming textbooks and zipping backpacks. "Some of you still need to sign up to discuss your essays. The list is on my office door."

Not a bad class today. Once he'd steered the lecture past the treacherous shoals of the class's incredulity that a Puritan woman could actually feel passion for her husband, most of the students seemed to engage with Anne Bradstreet's expressions of devotion and, yes, even fleshly longing for Simon's return from his business trip. Having one of the class's more attractive young women read the poem aloud had been an inspired move.

> Return; return, sweet Sol, from Capricorn;
> In this dead time, alas, what can I more
> Than view those fruits which through thy heat I bore?
> Which sweet contentment yield me for a space,
> True living pictures of their father's face.
> O strange effect! now thou art southward gone,
> I weary grow the tedious day so long;
> But when thou northward to me shalt return,
> I wish my Sun may never set, but burn
> Within the Cancer of my glowing breast,
> The welcome house of him my dearest guest.

How had one of the boys in the back row put it? "Dude, she's like, hot for him." Joe smiled. Sophie would've been so proud.

Joe wondered, not for the first time, if Simon Bradstreet had been appropriately appreciative of a wife who could not only feel such things but craft words that let others feel them, even four hundred years later.

He went back to his office. He sat down and thumbed the space bar on his keyboard, waiting until his computer woke from hibernation. He clicked the icon for his e-mail program. Ten new messages. Two were annoying spam from investment schemes, and one was the automated reminder from the university's payroll system to submit his vacation hours for the time between semesters. Joe shook his head. He was slightly amazed that the university's payroll system actually knew he existed.

A subject line caught his eye: "your Hawthorne paper." The sender was somebody with the user name "mckimmerk@iyu.edu." Joe clicked on the message.

Professor Barnes,

I'm Kevin McKimmer. I teach at Ira Young, a few hours west of you. (I Googled you and got your e-mail address from your university's Web site; hope you don't mind.) There's no reason you should remember me, but a few years ago (I've actually forgotten how many), I sat in on a

paper you gave at a regional conference of the Modern
Language Association, something along the lines of
"Hawthorne and the Rhetoric of Guilt."

As it happens, I've recently been appointed general editor
for a series our press here is putting together on American
literature before the Civil War. I'd really like to know what
else you've done on Hawthorne lately and whether you'd
have any interest in talking about a book proposal. We're a
scholarly press, of course, and very small, so nobody's getting rich, but if you'd be interested, I'd love to discuss it
with you.

Hoping to hear from you soon,

Kevin

Joe read the message twice, then sat back in his chair. He felt as if
the wind had been knocked out of him—but in a good way. Five
minutes ago he'd never heard of Kevin McKimmer, and now he
seemed like Joe's new best friend. What on earth might happen next?
He chuckled and shook his head.

"Good news, huh?"

He spun around. Alexis was standing in the doorway, smiling at
him in that offhand way he still found so unaccountably affecting.

"You wouldn't believe it if I told you."

"Try me."

He motioned her over to his computer screen and watched as she read the e-mail from Kevin McKimmer. She turned toward him and smiled.

"I love it when a plan comes together."

"Say what?"

"Just kidding," she said, laughing. "I'd enjoy taking credit for this, but some things are beyond the reach of even us deans."

"Don't say that. I'll lose all faith."

She gave him a playful look. "I doubt it."

"Touché." He got up from his desk.

"Where you headed?" she said.

"To lunch, I guess."

"Sounds good. Am I invited?"

"Are you asking as my dean?"

"Oh…why don't you think of it as coming from a friend?"

"A very good friend?"

"A very, very good friend."

Their faces were inches apart. Joe fought and conquered the urge to make sure the coast was clear. Instead he leaned in, and this time she didn't move away.

"If this keeps up, the streets will be dry before sunset," he said when they were in the car, backing out of his parking space.

"It was a short little freeze, wasn't it?"

Joe smiled. "It won't be the last."

"No. But let's just enjoy the sunshine while we have it."

Joe pulled out onto the street. He drove for a few seconds, then glanced across at her.

"I love you. You know that, don't you?"

"Without a doubt."

The point of view in which this tale comes under the romantic definition lies in the attempt to connect a by-gone time with the very present that is flitting away from us.

—NATHANIEL HAWTHORNE,
from the preface to *The House of the Seven Gables*

# NOTE TO READERS

The book of Job is, for me, one of the most troubling texts in the Bible. It begins with a bet between Jehovah and Satan. As if that picture weren't disturbing enough, the stakes of the wager, it turns out, are nothing less than a human life—actually, a number of human lives if you count the sons, daughters, and servants Job loses as a result of Satan's visitations. At first pass, Job's trials seem a rather harsh way to prove God's point.

This ancient text, though, exists in order to wrestle with one of mankind's oldest and most perplexing problems: why do the righteous suffer? It is a question that has produced reams of philosophy, theology, theater, and literature. It is an enigma that can keep a person awake through the wee hours. It is a bitter mystery for anyone who has ever watched a child struggling with a dread disease.

In Elie Wiesel's play *The Trial of God*, the Jews in a Nazi concentration camp actually carry out one of Job's wishes, as expressed in Job chapter 23: they bring a suit against God for his negligence toward them. Like Job, they accuse God of being absent in their suffering. In the end, God is found guilty. And what is the response of the plaintiffs after the successful prosecution of their lawsuit? They return to their prayers.

A few years ago I read Philip Yancey's *Disappointment with God,* in which the author explores the same sort of hard questions about God posed by Job and Wiesel: Is God unfair? Is God silent? Is God hidden? As I read, I ran across the quote that appears at the opening of this novel: "I had a strong sense that God doesn't care so much about being analyzed. Mainly, he wants to be loved." And that set me to thinking... What if God desires from me, from all his creation, something like what we desire from those we love? Doesn't each of us desire to be loved, as Yancey puts it, "for no good reason"? Don't we grow weary of relationships in which an accounting is constantly demanded, relationships based on the principle of quid pro quo, relationships that require us to do something in return for the benefits granted by the other party? What if God, having loved us with no strings attached, actually longs for us to love him the same way in return?

As my mind worked along these lines, I ran across a notion about the book of Job in a commentary I was reading. The gist was that a good way of understanding the book of Job is to see God, rather than Job, as the main character. That, combined with Yancey's comment, gave me the idea of constructing a retelling of Job that was framed as a love story between God and Job.

Now, admittedly, the love-story analogy is far from perfect, especially in this context. Like all analogies, it breaks down at certain points—hence, the cautionary words at the beginning from Paul Valéry. But like all good analogies, it does present certain useful hints and perspectives.

And, like the book of Job itself, this novel stops short of trying to answer the questions with which it grapples. As I read the ending of the book of Job, I find God, rather than justifying Job's suffering or even explaining the wager with Satan, simply saying in effect, "Job, I'm God, and you're not. I'm going to bless you now, but I'm not required to explain myself to you." And like the Jews in Wiesel's play, Job falls down in worship. End of story. I've tried to take my cue from the text of Job and leave a few questions unanswered, a few pages not completely colored in. I think that some stories function well by posing questions and inviting us to reflect on our own answers and perhaps even engage in a discussion of the mysteries that remain.

*Thom Lemmons*